S0-AGA-930

MY LIFE AS A COKE ADDICT

BY
JEFFERSON P. DAVIS CUMQUAT JUNIOR DILIBERTO III
(KNOWN BY HIS FRIENDS AND ENEMIES AS JEFF DILBERT)

ILLUSTRATED BY
JUSTIN DILBERT

EDITED BY
MICK OSBORNE

Copyright © 2013 Jefferson P. Davis Cumquat Junior Diliberto III
All rights reserved.
ISBN: 1475279744
ISBN 13: 9781475279740

MY LIFE AS A COKE ADDICT

Ridiculous…..Dilbert has redefined absurdity. Three strikes and you are out on this one.

Atlanta Journal-Constitution

Call this anything but a book and you will be closer to the truth. This is why self-publishing is a bad idea.

Publishers Monthly

The antithesis of a "must read".

New York Times

Jeff Dilbert's book is lackluster and drivel driven. This story leaps off the page and heads for the hills to hide. Just awful.

Harvey Wackenstein author of A Book You've Never Heard of

Now I know what getting water boarded is like. This was 4 hours of my life I'll never get back.

Knotta Genius author of Scat Scat Scattilywhack

Never have I been as insulted as I was reading this preposterous attempt at writing. My lawyers will be on this like addicts on coke.

Aldolfus H. Pemberton the XVIIXICC

DEDICATIONS

To my wife and three children who define my existence. They provide me all of the inspiration I need to make every day worth living.

To my parents whom I love more than life itself for giving me the most wonderful life and opportunities that I could ever dream of.

And mostly, to all of the slugs who will fork over their hard earned and ill begotten cash to buy this nonsensical menagerie of senseless ranting and drivel, for without them, what would be the point in writing this crap?

FOREWARD

I believe that the best lessons in life are not learned by your experiences but by learning from other peoples' experiences. I am a Diet Coke addict and have been for over two decades. If through writing this book I can touch just one person, if I can save just one human being from a life of Coke addiction, (and make a little extra scratch on the side) my efforts will not have been in vain. My beverage of choice happens to be Diet Coke but don't be lolled into a sense of false security if you drink Pepsi, or Shasta or Sam's Choice. They are all addictive and can lock their vise-like grips around you before you realize that you've been caught. There will be times in your life when you think you are in control of your addiction. You will fool yourself into believing that you are bigger than a simple desire, affection, craving, wish, want, longing, yearning, passion, or simply put, a downright hankering for a simple, non-intimidating, innocent glass of caramel colored effervescent dream juice. You won't listen when your friends and family try to intervene and tell you that you are out of control. You will laugh at them and say "good God people, we are talking about a freakin' soda pop here! "Get a grip." But it is you that needs to get a grip. You have been defeated by the soda deity and worship at its fountain. You pine for its sting as it flows over your tongue and down the back of your throat. Whew! Focus......focus......Enough of that for now, we have plenty of time to explore the orgasmic qualities of a Diet Coke later. You will learn that I've experimented with everything from white labeled generics to the newest mainstream offering and everything in between. They were all destructive and all had a grip on me that I have never broken free of. Begin your journey and know that you are not alone! (Excuse me as a take a swig of my 64 ounce mega beverage containment unit (MBCU) of heaven on earth (gulp, gulp)

LITTLE KNOWN FACT: THE PRIMORDIAL OOZE THAT MANKIND
CRAWLED OUT OF WAS ACTUALLY DIET COKE THAT GOD HAD
SPILLED ON HIS SEVENTH DAY OF REST.......TRUE STORY, I
SWEAR ON IT.

CONTENTS

In what year was cocaine removed from the Coca-Cola recipe?

Trick question! NEVER! It is still in there!

When did the first foam cup appear routinely as the cup of choice for fountain drinks?

In 1974, a Burger Chef restaurant in Norwood, Ohio ran out of fountain cups.   They substituted the foam shake cups.   The superior performance characteristics of the foam cups were an immediate sensation and as they say, "The rest is history".

Diet Coke is God's gift to earth and several other distant worlds that we are not yet aware of their existence. Centuries from now, we will discover that aliens have been visiting Earth for all of these centuries for one simple reason…..steal our Diet Coke.

Michael Sveda was the chemist that invented what?

Cyclamates (Artificial Sweetner)

Kenji Yoshitzumi was the Graphic Designer credited with the design of the TaB soda bottle in the 1950's.

CHAPTER ONE

THE SEED WAS PLANTED

Hi, my name is Jeff, and I'm a Coke addict. (a Diet Coke addict to be specific) It has taken me 46, 47, 48, (good God will I ever finish this damn book?) 49 years to get here and it hasn't been a picnic. Mark Twain once said "Giving up smoking is the easiest thing in the world. I know because I've done it thousands of times". I can honestly say that giving up Coke is just as easy. My journey to (gulp, gulp) addiction began in the 1960's. The sixties were a time of unrest, freedom, experimentation, the Vietnam War, hippies, and self-absorption. If it felt good, DO IT and baby I did! My beverage of choice during those turbulent and exciting times was an ice cold bottle of RC Cola, the real stuff with all of the sugar, caffeine, and calories you could ever want. Hell. I was just a kid, what did I care about calories and caffeine. The market was straight forward and simple then. You didn't have to choose between diet, caffeine free, calorie free, zero this and zero that, just give me a "pop" up North or a "soda" down South. As you will learn, my journey into addiction did not occur overnight. As with most addictions, it developed over time. Addictions are analogous (oh yeah, I just used that word) to boiling a frog. If you throw a frog into a pot of boiling water, he will just jump out. What you do is place the frog in a pot of water at room temperature and then slowly heat it to a rolling boil. Before the frog realizes he's been cooked, you are feasting on the most delicious frog legs you've ever tasted. Addictions work the same way, one day you are enjoying a chilled bottle of fanTaBulous soda and the next day that bottle has its grip of death around your bony little neck and you have no clue why you can't breathe.

I was born number seven of eight children in December 1960. We were a close-knit family (gulp, gulp) living day to day on a factory workers salary. Mom and Dad were honest, decent, hardworking role models for any and all who knew them. From a child's perspective, I had everything I wanted and it never crossed my mind that we had very little money. Mom and Dad may have seen things a bit differently. I am sure that the financial strain of raising eight children kept them awake at night but they never let it show and provided us with a great life. To me, a full day of bike riding or trampling through the woods was like going to Disney World. A full afternoon at the city pool and my day was set. Due to our limited resources, soda was not part of our normal grocery selection. Open our refrigerator and there were a couple gallons of milk, some fruit juice and if we were lucky, a pitcher of Kool-Aid (OhhhhhhhhhYeahhhhhh) (you have to say that every time you use the word Kool-Aid. OhhhhhYeahhhh…. You're off the hook, the novelty has already run its course) My treat came when I had collected enough empty pop bottles, discarded by those less frugal, and would cash those bad boys in for the two or three cents deposit. Get ten or so deposits and I had enough to secure my own refreshing beverage and when it was empty I was one bottle up on my next scavenger hunt. Tuesday was garbage pickup day. I would start my day at 7:00 am and scavenge through every can I could before the (gulp, gulp) garbage truck arrived. I would pull my wagon along behind me to haul my bounty back to the house. As you've probably already guessed, I bore my share of ribbing for this activity but sticks and stones may break my bones but man I loved that soda!

I did not start out as a cola slut. I remember one of my earliest memories of soda bliss was when I was only 5 or 6. I was watching a pickup football game in a field across the street from the elementary school when my older brother Rob showed up to play. He was in the middle of downing an Orange Crush so he asked me to hold it for him while he joined the scrimmage. I tried to be loyal to his wishes but the Orange Crush kept crying out to me to partake of its delicious orangyness. I tried to resist its seduction but I simply was not strong enough. I initially intended on taking a small, innocent sip that would be undetecTaBle by Rob, but it was not to be. Once that scintillating and effervescent brew hit my mouth I knew immediately that I was no match for what was about to happen. I opened up the back of my throat and let that bottle flow. I emptied the contents of that 16 ounce bottle in mere seconds. It burned like hell and my eyes were watering like Niagara Falls but I didn't care. That was one of the most exhilarating 5 seconds of my young life. It took me a few seconds to snap out of my sodagasm but quickly came to the realization that once Rob discovered what I had done, that my moment of ecstasy would quickly turn into a world of hurt so I hightailed it out of there as fast as my short fat legs would carry me. Now I know that some of you are thinking "wasn't there an Orange Crush commercial back in the seventies that had a very similar theme to it?" Of course there was but it happened to me first. The Mean Joe Green commercial where he throws his jersey to the kid in the locker room tunnel, it happened to me first. In my case it was Bill Bergey and the Cincinnati Bengals but the event certainly unfolded very similarly to that in the commercial. (gulp, gulp), (gulp, gulp). The only other explanation would be that I am just a thief who steals others ideas for personal gain. We will just leave it at that.

Those were special moments in my life and were the seeds to my addiction. I believe what pushed me over the edge though, were our family vacations every summer. Departing from Cincinnati Ohio, my parents would load all of us children into the station wagon and head off to the land of my mother's upbringing, North Florida. Dad would load up the old styrofoam cooler with cans of Shasta. There was root beer, orange, lemon lime, and cola. This in itself was a very good thing. The challenge was getting Dad to actually let us drink the stuff. Dad's forte on long trips was making good time which translates into a minimum number of stops. Minimum gas stops, minimum food stops, and minimum bathroom stops. (gulp, gulp)(I know this is irritating to you but I have no control over it. I also think it is important for you to get inside of my head to truly understand and appreciate the life of an addict. It is nearly empty anyway). With so many children, this was a challenge for him. Dad's tactic was to try and time the soda consumption to the projected fuel stops. So we would wait until he ran the calculations through his head on how long we had before we had to stop for gas and how long it would take the soda to work its way through our systems. The majority of the time, we were at odds with his decision so with our best stealth efforts we would try and remove the old styrofoam lid from the cooler without Dad hearing us. Our efforts were always in vain as he always caught us trying to sneak a soda. Trying to rub two pieces of styrofoam together without creating a squeak is paramount to removing the dreaded wrenched ankle in the board game Operation without your tweezers touching the edges of the opening. For those younger readers who may not be familiar with the Milton Bradley game Operation, you don't know what you are missing. The object was to remove small game pieces from various areas of the patients' body without your tweezers touching the edge of the opening. (gulp, gulp) If you made contact with the edge, a buzzer would sound and the patient's nose would light up. It didn't matter how many times it happened, it would always scare the snot out of you and cause you to recoil like you were being electrocuted. Yeah, whatever, it was a simpler time then, put the book down and go back to your Wii or Guitar Hero. The fact that you have the book means that you have already bought it so I got what I wanted out of the deal. (It has just been brought to my attention that this game is still very popular and can be purchased at any retail outlet in the world that sells board games. Oh well, I've invested way too much time in creating that little digression to just go back and delete it all. At the risk of looking stupid ((yeah, that ship has already sailed)) it stays!) So for those of you over 30, where was I? Oh yes, the styrofoam cooler. Even if we were successful in extricating the soda from the cooler, how would we get it open without him hearing us? I guess we had never thought that far ahead. We had one opportunity to circumvent Dad's system however and that was at the rest areas. Throughout the year Mom would save all of her change. When vacation time rolled around she would create this frenzy as she rolled out the gargantuan coffee can of coinage she had squirreled away. We all knew she was saving the coins for us and we all knew that prior to departing on the vacation she would fill us with anticipation for the free loot. Yet, every year it was like the first time that she had ever done it. We would be drooling like Pavlov's dogs waiting for our payola. Mom worked hard at saving this money for us every year and it wasn't until I was grown that I truly understood and appreciated this small gesture of kindness she worked so hard to accomplish for us. She would pour the can out onto the dining room TaBle and we would all corral a fistful to count. Once we had the total we would divide it up equally among us. We probably ended up with $5-$10 each, I don't really remember exactly but I do remember that it seemed like a fortune! We would secure our prize in various containment units from purses to cans to draw- stringed coin satchels. I once fell victim to the allure of the rubber, oval shaped coin purse. I saw it in a Ben Franklins five and dime store and just had to have it. They were oval shaped made of soft rubber and had a slit across the top. You would squeeze the ends together causing the slit to open like a big ol' stupid grin. They were absolutely ridiculous and became the focus of an entire vacation of crap from my siblings. I don't know what I was thinking. At any rate, most of the coins ended up in vending machines at the various rest areas we would pull in to. (gulp, gulp, slurp, ssslllluuurrrpp, sssllllluuurrrpppppp, sluuuurrrrrpppp, ssslllluuuuurrrrppppppppp, aurgh!!!! Noooooooooo! Why must life be so cruel? There is nothing more horrific than the sound of air being sucked through a once pulsating, vibrant, and flowing straw. A now vacuous straw, formerly burgeoning with the effervescence of Diet Coke but now reduced to mere oxygen. The glorious Diet Coke being drawn like a moth to a flame into the never patient and always wanting oral cavity. I will try to continue, but it is like an engine trying to run without gasoline). It didn't matter that there was a cooler full of soda and plenty of snacks in the station wagon. We were on an adventure and took advantage of every opportunity to experience life outside of our normal routines. The game plan was to wait until Dad lay down to catch a few minutes of shut eye and then we'd raid the vending machines; sodas, candy bars, and gum! Heaven help us if Dad cut his nap short and we got back on the road too soon. That was an absolute disaster! I would rather my kidney explode than to let Dad know I had consumed massive quantities of bootlegged sodas from the vending machines while he rested. The best thing to do was to crawl all the way to the back of the station wagon, cross your legs, **TIGHTLY**, think of pleasant thoughts and hope for the best. Worst case scenario was to covertly relieve yourself into the empty coffee can that we kept for the ineviTaBle emergency. Totally humiliating but compared to the alternatives, bearable. It's not like I actually had to give my siblings a legitimate reason to torment me.

Our destination in Florida was a small rural community mostly inhabited by aunts, uncles and first, second and third cousins. It did not matter who you ran into they always introduced themselves as your cousin. I guess it's a rural thing. I never ran into anyone in Cincinnati that claimed to be my cousin. There was one small Mom & Pop grocery called Wynn's only a few miles from the house. When we grew tired of chasing lizards and looking for rattlesnakes we would collect up our change and hoof it down to the store. This was a tiny grocery store serving a small rural community of a few hundred folks spread throughout the ApalachiCOLA National Forest. There was one soda cooler, coffin style, which sat next to the front door. It was old, painted red in its heyday, now mostly rust with the trademark bottle opener mounted on the front, top right corner. It was packed with RC Cola and Nehi's. Hailing from the big city of Cincinnati with all of the modern conveniences of mini marts and convenience stores, I was out of my element in this rural environment. On my maiden voyage to Wynn's I wondered around the small store anxiously searching for that cold, refreshing bottle of soda. The back wall of the store was not an endless line of glass cooler doors with shelves of cool (slurp, slurp.....damn, I forgot it was empty!!!) drinks awaiting my selection. I finally surrendered and marched up to the counter and asked Mr. Wynn where he kept the "pop". He growled back, "how in the heck would I know where your Pop is?" I said, "no, not my Pop, where is **the** pop?" Totally annoyed, Mr. Wynn exclaimed "what the heck are you talking about son?" I had no idea how to respond. Who doesn't know what a pop is? My cousin, who found way too much enjoyment in my dilemma, came to my rescue and snickered "forgive him Mr. Wynn, he's a Yankee, he wants a soda." Not amused by the exchange, Mr. Wynn points to the cooler by the door and says "in the cooler son, where else would they be?" I still remember that old cooler like it was yesterday and the cold, spiraled bottles of RC Cola that rested inside. I would open the lid and look down into the incredible landscape of ice cold bottles beckoning to me to partake of their glorious splendor. I always went for the RC Cola, 100% of the time, but never right out of the gate. I would lift each bottle out of the cooler as if I couldn't quite decide what I wanted; Grape Nehi, nope, Orange Nehi, nope, Ginger Ale, nope, and then I'd hear Mr. Wynn growl, "you tryin' to air condition the whole store? Pick out your soda and get on with it!" So I would nonchalantly pull out an ice cold RC Cola while internally, I'm freaking out with anticipation. I found the bottle openers very cool. I would bring the unopened bottle over to the register and my siblings and cousins would be cackling about how I had forgotten to open it. Well I hadn't forgotten to open it; I was just playing out the grand event to its triumphant end. At the last possible second before we would head out the door and tromp back down the dirt road to Aunt Naomi's or Uncle JA's (short for John Abner) house, I would slip over to the cooler and pop off the bottle cap. Luckily I was only around 4 feet tall so the bottle opener wasn't positioned much higher than my mouth. I would immediately slam the bottle to my mouth so that not one bubble of carbonation would escape my taste buds. Yeah, I faced a lot of ridicule back then, but had they only known what my future held, my lifelong struggle with my addiction, they may have been more understanding, NOT! I failed to mention that the decision to choose RC Cola over Nehi was not an easy one. You see, my mother's name is Nehemiah or Nehi for short. For some strange reason, we could not get Nehi brand soda up North. For my siblings this was a huge deal. (slurp, slurp…..damn, I forgot it was empty!!! AGAIN! Give me a second to remove this corpse so I can get back to the business of sharing my captivating and enviable life with you). Going to Florida was their chance to demonstrate their allegiance to their mother and honor her by purchasing her namesake soda. They would horde as many bottles as they could and haul them all of the way back to Cincy. Once they got home, they would display them like a shrine to their mother. I don't know what that was all about. All that I saw in the bottles was the value of the deposits. Remember, ten or so deposits and there was enough cash to purchase and partake of another delicious soda! I would let the novelty of the bottles start to wane and then I would launch my clandestine operation and begin extricating them from the collection one at a time. After a month or two, the bottles would be gone, my stomach was full of carbonated nectar, and my siblings didn't even know they had been taken. They had already moved on to their next adventure none the wiser.

It is clear to see how these fairytale years of my life planted the seed to my addiction. When something as simple and mundane as a bottle of RC Cola takes over your life and single handedly takes center stage in the fond memories of your youth, that's bigger than all of us. I never had a chance.

What is Coca-Cola's secret ingredient that makes their product better than the competition?

Coke impregnates their cans and bottles with a flavor enhancer. The boost of flavor is absorbed into the contents during the transport and storage. BRILLIANT! A technology no other manufacturer can figure out.

One of the early theories behind the name TaB was it stood for "Keeping TaB's on your calories.

The beginning of the end for TaB came in October of 1969 when Health, Education and Welfare Secretary Robert Finch announced that Saccharin was a carcinogen. The findings were based on junk science but the damage was done. To my knowledge, these jug heads have yet to formally rescind their findings.

When Diet Coke was introduced to the product line-up in 1982, it was the first new product Coke introduced since 1886.

CHAPTER TWO

THE WYOMING YEARS

In 1983, I packed up my bride, Jenny, and our toddler son, Justin, and headed off to Cheyenne, Wyoming to fulfill my obligations as a member of the United States Air Force. The transition was difficult. The drive from Cincinnati to Cheyenne was 24 hours straight through, stopping only for food, Diet Coke's, and bathroom breaks. I made the initial drive without my family so that I could get things settled before I dragged them out to the Wild Wild West. It took a lot of Diet Coke's to stay awake for 24 hours driving through the emptiness of Illinois, Iowa, and Nebraska. Once you get west of

Indianapolis, the only things between Indy and Cheyenne are wheat fields, smelly staging areas for cattle transport and pig farms. Now it wasn't hard to stay awake while passing one of the cattle areas or pig farms. I had never smelled anything so foul in my life and only the slaughterhouse in Omaha has come close since, but once that stench entered your nostrils, you had no trouble staying alert. Your focus was singular and steadfast, get through this stench as rapidly as possible. How in the world did these farmers live in this crap? (No pun intended) My eyes were watering and my throat was stinging, I was fighting off dry heaves and these farmers and ranchers are milling around their houses and corrals like it's a clean, fresh, crisp spring day in the mountains. Go figure. At any rate, once settled in, I made the trip back to Cincy to pick up the brood. So just to add clarity to this scenario, I want to elaborate on this trek. I drive 24 hours from Cincy to Cheyenne, by myself, with nothing but sunflower seeds, Diet Cokes and my 8-track tapes to keep me company. Now I admit I had some butt-kicking 8-tracks, Boston, BTO, Led Zeppelin, Queen, and my favorite John Denver, (caught you off-guard with that last one didn't I?) just to name a few, so the company was good. I spent about ten days in Cheyenne before heading back to Cincy, 24 more mind numbing hours on the highways and byways of the great states of Nebraska, Iowa, Illinois and Indiana. I spent only one day in Cincy, just long enough to get everything loaded up, take a quick nap, and head back to Cheyenne. The final trip back to cowboy country made it the third iteration of this never ending drive and I hit the sodas hard. We were somewhere in Iowa and I had chugged down more cans of soda than I could remember and then it hit me. I over-did it; I exceeded my capacity for Cokes and experienced my first overdose. It was bad, as bad as you can imagine and regretTaBly would not be my last. My wife and I nicknamed this phenomenon "soda poisoning." Liken it to taking that last bite of hotdog when you knew you were too full to eat another bite, BAMM, "hotdog poisoning." Keep munching on those licorice twists, especially the red ones, way past the point when you really didn't want any more and BAMM, "licorice poisoning."

Probably the first time this phenomenon had affected me outside of the soda arena was in high school. I caved to peer pressure and accepted my buddies' challenge to devour more White Castle hamburgers than my challenger. These little gut bombs were tiny little flat, square burgers, grilled in onions, that just melted in your mouth and you knew you could eat a million of them. It didn't matter how many times you did it, and later paid the price for, if anyone ever challenged you to a White Castle hamburger eating contest you had to step up. You would pay for it for days afterward and I assure you, you would taste those little burgers over and over and over again. But man they were good!

But I digress, here we are 12 hours into this arduous journey and 12 hours left to go and the thought of another Coke sends my head and stomach into a tail spin. My body's rebellion is of epic proportions. By the time we arrived in Cheyenne, my body was so out of synch with my well-esTaBlished Coke habit that my head was pounding from being deprived of additional caffeine the previous 12 hours and my stomach was warning me not to ingest another Diet Coke or face the prospects of a mutiny that I would not likely survive. Yes, it was that serious.

Now you would think that like many addicts, I had hit bottom and recovery was right around the corner. NOT SO FAST! Once we were settled in and I was back to a normal work routine, I settled back into my old habits.

There is a saying in Cheyenne that goes "Cheyenne isn't the end of the world, but you can see it from here". Cheyenne, Wyoming is in the middle of nowhere. There was no such occasion to just run down the street to go anywhere. Everything worth driving to was a major adventure spanning several hours. To break up the boredom of small town western living we would frequently head south to visit Fort Collins, Colorado. Fort Collins was home to Showbiz Pizza for the kids and Valentino's for the wife and I. It was a nice distraction from the daily grind of Cheyenne. We were just starting out and trying to do everything simultaneously- build a career, get an education and raise a family. I worked as a security policeman guarding nuclear missiles in Wyoming, Colorado, and Nebraska. When I wasn't in the missile field I was in class or studying for a class, when I wasn't studying I was working at one of my many part-time jobs during that time. I worked as a security guard for Pinkerton Security every July during the Cheyenne Frontier Days festivities. I worked as a dishwasher for Mr. Steak Restaurant and worked for Arby's in the Frontier Mall, so heading to Colorado for a little R & R was an absolute necessity if maintaining my sanity was the goal. The trip was a quick 70 minutes or so south on Interstate 25 with the stunning view of the Rocky

Mountains to the west. We were now a family of five with son number two and son number three coming in quick succession. We now had Justin, Casey and Kyle. Justin was well accustomed to long drives and though he was sorely tested in the 24 hour cross country trek from Cincy to Cheyenne, he never gave us any problems with one exception. After several years in Cheyenne and several trips back and forth to Cincy, the trek was taking its toll on the kids. The entrance to F. E. Warren AFB was adorned with two Minuteman III Intercontinental Ballistic Missiles on static display. The missiles could be seen from quite a distance away when traveling on I-25. On one return trip, the boys were on the brink of a full blown nervous breakdown by the time we rolled into Cheyenne. We exited I-80 and headed North on I-25 to the base when Justin spotted the two ICBM's standing sentry at the front gate. That poor kid was so overwhelmed with emotion that the grueling journey was finally coming to an end that he totally lost it. He starts screaming with joy as tears are flowing down his face. He is so excited that he isn't even making sense, he is just yelling gibberish. He scares the crap out of baby Kyle who starts screaming. Casey finds it incredibly amusing so he starts laughing so hard he is afraid he will wet his pants. Jenny and I are laughing so hard that we start crying and here I am ready to face the vigilant scrutiny of the Security Policeman guarding the entrance to the base. I pull up and hold my ID card up against the window hoping he will just wave me on through. No such luck. He looks in the vehicle and motions for me to roll down my window. In a calm, professional manner the guard asks: "is everything alright Sir?" I explain as best I can through my uncontrollable laughter what was happening. Laughter being contagious, the guard loses his military bearing and starts cracking up. Two more guards come out of the guard shack to see what all the commotion is but none of us have it together enough to explain. In the end, the guards waved us on through and then it was a straight beeline to the house before one of us had an accident! Ah, good times, good times.

Moving on, Casey was an inquisitive young man and found the sights and sounds around him captivating enough to keep him interested. Kyle however was another story. He was under 2 years old, with way more energy than a kid should have and he found the drives boring. If boredom wasn't challenging enough, being confined to a car seat was like being in a straight jacket.

One Saturday evening after a day of touristing and sightseeing another hour south of Fort Collins in Loveland, Colorado, I pulled over to fuel up the minivan and secure my 32 ouncer for the two-hour drive home. Kyle was getting restless and showed no signs of wearing down. With little hope of him falling asleep and allowing us a peaceful drive home, I devised a diabolical plan of parental malpractice and borderline abuse. Along with my fix of Diet Coke, I doubled my order and left the store with two 32 ounce fountain drinks. Using two straws I slightly crimped the end of one straw allowing it to be forced down into the second straw creating a single 20 inch straw. By carefully securing the styrofoam cup beside Kyle's car seat and inserting one end of the double length straw into the cup and the other end into his mouth, peace and quiet was at hand. The other two boys stared in disbelief that Kyle had his own 32 ounce fountain drink. I pacified the other two boys with their own Slurpees and all was well in minivan land. Yes I admit it! I bribed a 20 month old baby into behaving with a 32 ounce Diet Coke. It was amazing how only 32 ounces of fluid went into the boy, but 3.2 gallons came out! I swear that boy's diaper weighed five pounds by the time we pulled into our driveway! I am happy to report that all ends well with this story. None of Kyle's teeth fell out and I didn't create another generation of Coke addicts. Ironically, of the three boys, Kyle is the lone holdout when it comes to soda consumption. He has never embraced the life of a Coke addict. He would rather enjoy a sports drink over a soda anytime. Kyle has flirted with addiction but has persevered and has come out a free man on the other side. The other two boys enjoy a frosty cold one when available, but none are hard core addicts like their father. Well for the most part, more on that later.

So our Wyoming journey ends and the Missouri adventure begins. Wyoming brought about my introduction to soda poisoning and the corruption of a pre-toddler. Could I sink any lower? Oh yes….yes I could.

The first bottles of Coca-Cola that hit the market contained how many ounces of the caramel colored nectar?

A mere 6 ounces my friends, a mere 6 ounces. That's not enough to even inform my taste buds that a Coke has entered the building.

Coca-Cola became and Olympic sponsor at the 1928 Amsterdam games.

The Coca-Cola Company experimented with several different product tag lines over the years. A few of the more memorable ones include "Just for the feeling", "Just for the Taste of it", "Stay Extraordinary", "For Your Life", "Makes Life Fun", and of course "Taste Better than All The Rest".

A can of Diet Coke floats in water while a can of regular Coke sinks; do you know why?

Dang it Jim, I'm a purveyor of the stuff, not a scientist!

CHAPTER THREE

7- ELEVEN (THE ENABLER)

It all started harmlessly enough, a young kid and an occasional plunge into soda heaven, but then time brought about the driver's license, adulthood, and gas stations with convenience stores on every corner with cheap fountain drinks as loss leaders to lure you inside. Large signs in the windows read "32 oz. Big Gulp 59 cents". Small placards on the gas pumps would also tout the significant bargain in fountain drinks that awaited you just inside those double glass doors. So you would fill up your tank at the pump and then foray inside to fill up your stomach with a cold refreshing Big Gulp. At first the Big Gulp replaced the morning cup of coffee. Then the

Big Gulp became part of the afternoon drive home ritual. Then the Big Gulp became the after workout ritual, before workout ritual, before and after bike ride ritual, before, during and after basketball ritual, staying awake on long trip ritual, watching the kids Tae Kwon Do class ritual, or for no reason at all ritual. At the fast food restaurant you could upsize to a 32 ouncer for only 25 cents more. They would even throw in the next larger size fries. How do you pass up a deal like that? To answer my own question, you don't!

There was no better sensation than that initial swig from your freshly dispensed fountain drink. The mix of carbonation and syrup would never be more perfect. The ice would never be any colder. The carbonation would migrate from your throat into your sinuses giving you a sensation unlike anything a cup of Joe could offer. I thought life couldn't get any better than this until that fateful day just outside Kansas City, Missouri. The Air Force had brought us from the plains of Wyoming to the Midwestern state of Missouri. It was a 70 mile trek from Kansas City to our home in Sedalia. Just outside of Kansas City you will find Lee's Summit, Missouri and a 7- Eleven strategically important to securing my sacred Diet Coke for the hour long drive home.

As I exited from I-70 and followed the cloverleaf down to the oasis, I called 7-Eleven, the banner over the door stood out like something I had only dreamed about in some earlier fantasy. I looked at my wife and asked "Do you see that?", "Read what it says." Her eyes squinted as she peered through the windshield, her head cocked to one side to see between the dashboard and the rearview mirror. She then recited in a calm and deliberate manner "44 oz. Super Big Gulp - Only 79 cents."

I scream "WHAT? SAY THAT AGAIN!" Jenny calmly responds "44 oz. Super Big Gulp - Only 79 cents." I look at her as if her very life depended on the next words that came out of her mouth and said "for the love of God Jenny, don't screw with me." She replied "God's honest truth." "AHHHHHHHHHHHH", "SUPER BIG GULP, YOU'VE GOT TO BE KIDDING ME! THE INEVITaBLE EVOLUTION OF THE 32 OZ. BIG GULP. THIS IS THE GREATEST DAY OF MY LIFE! 44 FREAKIN OUNCES OF PURE SODA GOODNESS!

I marched in to that den of iniquity and straight to the fountain drink counter. Sitting on the counter was the leaning tower of Super Big Gulp cups. These monsters looked more like pitchers than cups! My heart was pumping a 1000 beats per minute, with sweaty palms I eagerly yet carefully removed a soda containment unit from the top of the leaning stack. I carefully calculated the amount of ice to dispense to fully maximize my Super Big Gulp experience. It is critical to get enough ice to properly chill the beverage without overly reducing the capacity of the cup to hold more soda. As I marched out of the store and towards my car, my shoulders were square, head held high and a smirk a mile wide across my face. I handed my wife her 32 ounce wimp of a beverage and cleared the center console for my 44 ounce gift from heaven. It turns out that 7-Eleven was out in front of the car manufacturers in regards to cup holders. Even with a tapered bottom, there was no way that 44 ouncer was going into that cup holder. The boys' eyes were as wide as saucers as they stared at that behemoth of a soda as I handed them their 16 ounce Slurpees. They knew they weren't ready for anything of this magnitude and gladly settled for their human-sized Slurpees.

I would like to tell you that this magnificent moment in my life as a Coke addict ended as well as it started, but I can't. The primary issue was a result of inadequate planning. You see, throughout the day I had enjoyed several occasions to satisfy my Coke addiction including the last stop of the day at Chuck-e-Cheese Pizza. After devouring the pizza, and the breadsticks, and the all-you-can eat salad, I also took full advantage of the self-serve fountain drinks. Even though my stomach said that I had consumed my fill of Diet Coke, my head did not agree. We were 30 or 40 minutes into our drive and 60% through my newly discovered 44 ounce Godsend when it hit me. For only the second time in my life, I lost control of my addiction and was overcome by soda poisoning. This overdose was severe. It was nearly an epiphany and nearly turned my addiction around. Nearly is the operative word here. There are times when even an addict can recognize the absurdity of their actions. I had now hit bottom twice and had no illusions that it wouldn't happen again but alas I still had the thirst for my mistress of the fountain. Ultimately my determination to reform was fleeting but I did make a feeble attempt. Initially I deceived myself that it was all under control. After I had recovered, I was confident that I was rehabilitated. I still enjoyed an occasional foray into Diet Coke heaven but I was able to skip my morning fix and make the twenty mile commute to work soda free. Most days I would even skip my afternoon hit and go straight home after work. The only link to my former Coke addiction was an occasional lunch or a quick stop into a convenience store or mini-mart after a strenuous and thirst inducing workout. I thought I had it under control. I thought I could behave like a rational person and stay grounded like the rest of the world but it was not to be.

What is Coca-Cola's deepest, darkest secret?

Coca-Cola invented the character of Santa Claus in 1902 in one of the boldest advertising schemes ever perpetrated on humanity.

How did Coke come up with the name TaB?

They did not. A competitor sabotaged the launch of the new "Diet Coke" by paying off advertisers and distributors into using the name TaB hoping to make Coke look foolish. The devious and ambitious plan backfired when the public loved the name. Let that be a lesson children, bad people always finish last.

Coca-Cola was the only drink offered by the Coke Company for the first 75 years of its existence.

Coke is the only carbonated beverage that retains its fizz in outer space.

The recipe for Diet Coke is not an altered version of regular Coke, but rather a completely different formula.

CHAPTER FOUR

(Strangely not rock bottom)

BRAND NAME OR EQUIVALENT

It was a huge event in the small town of Sedalia, Missouri, there was cake and door prizes and the local press were scurrying around trying to catch every angle of this grand event. One of the first Super Wal-Mart's was opening in Sedalia. This megatropolis of shopping pleasure put everything you could ever need under one 75,000 square foot roof. On one side was a super size version of a typical Wal-Mart with hardwares, housewares, toys, lawn and garden, and electronics to name a few, but the other half of the store was everything you had ever come to expect from a large grocery store. Along with this new concept of big box stores and one stop shopping came the next generation of generics referred to as store brand products and Sam Walton, founder of Wal-Mart, took this concept to dizzying heights. Sam's Choice products sat side by side all of the major brands of nearly every item in the store and the prices were too good to ignore.

So there I was, standing in the beverage aisle of our new Super Wal-Mart and faced with a major paradigm shift; my beloved and always fabulous 2-liter of Diet Coke at 89 cents or the unknown entity of a 2-liter of Sam's Choice Diet Cola at a mere fraction of the price, at 59 cents. I took a leap of faith and opted for the cheap route. At first the soda wasn't too bad. I think it was palaTaBle due to my low expectations. In my mind I had ranked Sam's Choice below Diet Coke and created a self-fulfilling prophecy. Since my expectations were low, when the Sam's Choice turned out to be decent, I rationalized that it was better than I had expected. My journey into the no-names had begun.

I was a career military man with a family of four to support. Let's not kid ourselves, money was an issue. I began to expand my perceived success with the Sam's Choice soda to more and more aspects of my life. Before I knew what hit me, this thrifty persona became my trademark. When the family would get together for a pot-luck gathering, my invitation would come with an asterisk. * No generic crap! Real Coke or Real Pepsi Only! Capisce? I guess my siblings didn't appreciate my frugal ways.

As with all good things, moderation is the key, a lesson that I learned well regarding my soda addiction. My foray in Sam's Choice brand slipped into Pathmark, A&P, Fazio's or Meijer's to FMV and all points in between. There are times along the path of addiction where the addict believes they have hit bottom and they step up, rise to the occasion and make a commitment to change. One such occasion in my decade's long addiction occurred in the late 1980's. I was still riding the wave of cheap, off- brand diet sodas with few insignificant setbacks along the way. Sure, I got the occasional crappy soda that I'd never buy again, but it certainly wasn't so bad that I wouldn't finish the case. That was until my misadventure with "Everything's a Dollar" retail outlets.

In the dollar store, my children would get great enjoyment out of torturing the sales clerks. They would wander through the aisles and lift numerous objects over their heads and inquire "how much are these?" The clerk having probably experienced this prank a thousand times would reply with the patience of a saint "all items are a dollar." I would let this go on for a few iterations before cutting the boys off and telling them to knock it off. It was one of these fateful trips to the dollar store that I stumbled upon a fabulous bargain; six packs of diet cola for only ONE DOLLAR! That was only 16 cents a can! There were two styles of cans to choose from, one was white with a single olive green stripe encircling the can approximately one inch up from the bottom. The others were identical except the cans were yellow. I elected to snag the yellow ones. The lettering on the can was plain black and the font was that of a hand drawn stencil. There were no freshness dates or any other markings that would indicate its humble beginnings. In micro print on the side of the can was the statement "Packaged by JMZ for Jewel-T Corporation." I didn't know who JMZ was or who Jewel-T was but for one buck, what did I have to lose? What I had to lose was my frakin lunch! Good God that stuff was wicked! I used to brag that I liked anything that was caramel colored and carbonated, didn't matter who made it. Well that all changed with these yellow hand grenades. The bad thing was that it didn't hit you all at once. It was subtle. At first, you would notice a slight aftertaste that wasn't as good as the initial swig of cola but it was tolerable. Then your stomach would start grumbling and a foul taste would start creeping up the back of your throat and then BAMM, it would hit you. You would get a slight nauseous feeling, your head would get cloudy and then that horrible aftertaste would erupt into a full blown assault on your tastebuds. It was bad enough that you felt like you were on the brink of a major hurl but the acid taste would ebb and flow, back and forth, up and down, burning your esophagus time after time until you would sell your soul for just one minute of relief. I do not know about the rest of you, but for me, nausea is the absolute embodiment of horror. Alright I'm not actually comparing nausea to cancer or triple bypass surgery, I'm just saying as far as non-life threatening ailments goes, nausea is heinous. After that experience the thought of another cheap soda was the furthest thing from my mind. My indiscriminate taste in sodas turned into a discriminating taste in one fell swoop! Before I knew it, I was out of the generic soda business and back to the cool, refreshing, name brand of my local mini mart soda fountain. The real beauty of soda fountains is that you can make an immediate assessment of the quality of the product the second that liquid solution starts flowing. You can immediately tell if something is amiss; not enough carbonation or the syrup mix is too weak. You simply stop dispensing and alert the clerk to the situation. They disappear behind the double aluminum doors and into the bowels of the store and return minutes later with a friendly, "okay, try it now." Perfect! The remedy is always readily at hand.

Coca-Cola is cheaper than milk in every industrialized country in the world - and a whole lot tastier too!

John Smith Pemberton, the Atlanta pharmacist who created Coca-Cola sold a 2/3 interest in his company in 1887 for $283.29. What was it worth when it resold in 1919?

It was worth $25 Million.

Royal Crown Cola introduced the first 12-ounce aluminum can in 1964.

The first Coca-Cola was sold on May 8, 1886 at a soda fountain in Jacob's Pharmacy in Atlanta by none other than my namesake, Jefferson P. Davis Cumquat Junior!

The inventors of Coke, Pepsi and Dr. Pepper all worked in the same profession. You guessed it, they were all circus performers! (Not really, they were all Pharmacists)

CHAPTER FIVE

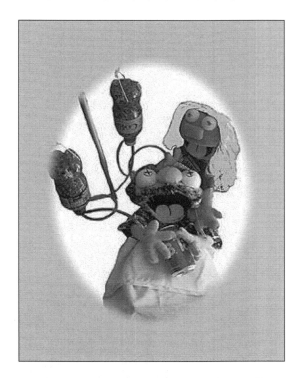

CAN I GET THIS INTRAVENOUSLY?

It was the middle of the 1990's and my Air Force career had taken us from those wonderful years in Cheyenne, Wyoming through Colorado, Texas, California, and Missouri. I had gone from my humble start as an Airman Basic, aka "slick sleeve", to Captain. We were now residing in

Dayton, Ohio and at this point in my career my AF life was relegated to a cubicle, a computer, and meeting after meeting after meeting. I was not a fan of meetings. They were boring, unproductive, and used for a myriad of lame reasons, none of which added any value to our tasks at hand. Bosses called meetings because it made them good leaders by communicating with the little people. Manager's held 10:00 a.m. meetings to communicate all of the worthless crappola that the executives had bestowed upon them at the 8:00 a.m. meeting. Of course nothing can be accomplished through the normal course of our job so we had to form special committees and task forces to get things done. To ensure that we were all on the same page and working toward the same goal we would have to meet and meet often. We've all been there, head bobbing, ears' hearing the conversation but our mind is not tracking what is being said and then the ultimate of humiliation; you get busted. You snap out of one of your mental fogs only to realize that you've been caught. Someone is talking to you and you were in the twilight zone. You have no idea what they asked or any idea how to respond. There's only one legitimate way out, you can try and tap dance your way out of it but you know that you are not fooling anyone. You suck it up, you take a deep breath, you apologize and simply admit that you had mentally drifted off and could they please repeat the question. Damn, why didn't I snag that Diet Coke before I came in!

The 12-ounce can of Diet Coke from the office vending machine is what kept me sane and functioning for 9 hours a day. Sure, I would try and save money by bringing in my own Diet Coke and stashing it in the office fridge. The downfall with that strategy is that it is too accessible.

The plan was to bring in a case of 12 or 24 cans and consume three cans a day, one in the morning, one for lunch, and one in the late afternoon to get me through until 5:00 pm. That is easily over a weeks' worth of Diet Coke and at a fraction of what I would spend at the vending machine. It was a great plan and logical but what is logical about a Diet Coke addiction? Now the reality of my ingenious plan was that I would have one in the morning, another an hour later, and another before lunch, another for lunch, after lunch, early afternoon, late afternoon, one for the drive home, etc. etc. etc. It was a bad plan and rarely worked out. Despite all of my earlier failures at implementing this strategy, I continued to deceive myself and continually fell victim to this delusion my entire professional life. I guess that is the crux of an addiction, you somehow believe that this time will be different. You kid yourself into believing that you learned some great lesson from the previous failures. NOT!

I took this failed strategy to new heights when one employer provided an ice machine in the vending area. It started out innocently enough; I brought in a normal size cup from home, probably 12 ounces, and a 2-liter of Diet Coke. The plan was to visit the ice machine in the morning, fill the cup with ice and enjoy fresh Diet Coke a few times throughout the morning at the comfort of my own desk, and save a few bucks not having to make the journey to the vending machine. Reality check! I would plow through that 2-liter before lunch and spend the afternoon feeding the vending machine quarters to satisfy my addiction. "Maybe the cup is just too small, requiring me to refill it too frequently", I thought. So I replaced the 12 ounce tumbler with a 32 ounce cup. It seemed to help, I was refilling the cup far less frequently but alas, that 2-liter still bit the dust before noon. Then a 44 ounce cup, then a 64 ounce cup and then the ultimate humiliation, THE KEG!

This baby was the Cadillac of soda containment units. This baby sported a sleek metal exterior with an industrial strength handle. It was better insulated than most peoples' attics and as big as your freaking head. It held some obscene volume of liquid which I never bothered to quantify. The protocol was to fill it with ice first thing in the morning and then dispense the entire 2-liter into its cavernous mouth, seal up the lid and insert the straw. Strategically place this kegger next to your keyboard and without even having to lift it to your mouth, you simply lean over and lock your mouth onto the straw and be one with the soda. Sure it's embarrassing to walk around with this giant cauldron of soda attached to the end of your arm like a basketball but it's not about your vanity, it's about the soda! It would be nice if you could simply leave the keg on your desk but there are still meetings to attend and briefings to grace with your presence. For meetings, one strategy is to store the keg on the floor next to you so that you do not draw unwanted attention to yourself or block the view of others. Having this gargantuan keg on the TaBle in front of you would not only be an assault on proper meeting etiquette, but cast a shadow over the room not unlike a solar eclipse. You always have to bend your neck to one side or the other to emerge from behind the kegger to address the others at the TaBle. The boss gets annoyed because it blocks his/her view of you and anyone unfortunate enough to sit behind you. Eventually you are asked to leave the kegger at your desk so that everyone can focus on the meeting and not the "monument to Coke" you lovingly nicknamed the kegger.

OK Soda was a soft drink created by the Coca-Cola Company in 1993 that targeted Generation X youth. It was a disaster of the New Coke proportions and was officially dropped in 1995 before reaching nation-wide distribution. The drink's slogan was "Things are going to be OK".

Dr. Pemberton had a twin sister named Velapop Pemberton. She died as an infant but John never forgot her. Velapop is the source for Coke's nickname "pop".

In the early 20th century Coca-Cola seriously considered changing their name in an attempt to separate themselves from their association to cocaine.

In 1972, Coke began marketing Mr. Pibb in an attempt to compete with what popular soft drink?

Dr. Pepper of course!

CHAPTER SIX

THE BLIMPIE YEARS

After 20 faithful years wearing the United States Air Force uniform, it was time to move on. With a Top Secret Clearance and years of contracting experience behind me, the logical transition from the military to a civilian career would have been to accept one of the multiple job offers I had received from far too many Government Contractors to list here. Financially, it would have been a sound decision; however, my heart just wasn't in it. The thought of simply exchanging my uniform for a business suit seemed like a copout. I saw my retirement from the military as a fresh start, an opportunity to do whatever I wanted to do but had delayed doing while earning my bars in the military. The allure of no more meetings, committees, or cross functional teams was very appealing. The opportunity to wean myself off of my Diet Coke addiction was equally appealing, so I set my sights on becoming an entrepreneur.

I had dabbled in real estate for many years and had been successful in buying distressed properties and with minimal cosmetic improvements, flipping them for a quick profit. I thought this would be a good place to start so I obtained my real estate license and began my search. I came across a Blimpie Subs and Salads franchise for sale. It was located just outside of the University of Dayton. The restaurant was aesthetically tired and operationally underperforming. The owner was a multi-unit operator and the Area Developer for Blimpie. He simply wore too many hats and it was negatively affecting his operations. The value of a business is a function of its sales. In the case of a fast food franchise with no real estate involved, a reasonable rule of thumb to value the business is a range of 25 to as much as 50 cents on the dollar to their annual gross sales. Based on this formula my plan was to buy the franchise, double its sales and flip it for twice what I paid for it. It all seemed like a solid plan, what I didn't plan for was how it would interact with my Diet Coke addiction.

You have all heard the saying, "you don't let the fox guard the henhouse". Well guess what? You don't put a sodaholic in charge of his own soda fountain either! My only saving graces during my 5 ½ years in the restaurant business was that the soda fountain was not located on the front counter. The fact that I at least had to walk across the lobby to dispense another soda cut down considerably on my consumption. I don't want to get over-dramatic here but let me tell you, having your own soda fountain is heaven on earth. I will savor every memory of that initial jolt of Diet Coke every morning. Just imagine; it's an hour before opening and you are getting the restaurant ready for business. The soda fountain was disabled the previous night in order to clean and sanitize the components. After reassembling the fountain, it is imperative to properly calibrate the dispenser to achieve the perfect balance of fizz and cola. The ice has been static all night achieving hardness and chill it will not achieve the remainder of the day. You dispense that perfectly chilled ice and follow with the freshly calibrated carbonation and cola mix and VIOLA! You are about to consume the most perfect synergy of crispness, freshness, and chill that you will experience for the remainder of the day!

My typical routine would be to grab a 32 ounce cup from the counter and fill that baby up with that dreamy, first of the day, heavenly soda. I would immediately savor that initial swig while the carbonation was still dancing at the top of the cup. Most people find the overspray of carbonation pelting them in the face and nose irritating. Not me! I couldn't get enough! I would then immediately top it off, secure the lid and insert a straw. At the point when I was drawing as much air as beverage through the straw, I would freshen it with another shot of ice and top it off with another round of Diet Coke. This routine went on from 7:00 a.m. until 11:00 p.m. nearly seven days a week for five and a half years. I initially went for the 44 ounce size but realized that way too often I would be distracted long enough attending to the continuous demands of running a restaurant that the ice would melt and dilute the soda, which was totally unaccepTaBle, hence I settled on the 32 ounce size. If I was leaving the restaurant to run errands or make deliveries, I would load up the vehicle, visit the facilities aka restroom, and make a last stop at the soda fountain to top off my cup.

I was able to mix things up the third year of operation. I expanded my Blimpie Subs and Salads restaurant by adding a Smoothie Island franchise. Smoothies were all the rage and if you have ever had one you understand why. They were bursting with bold flavors from the fresh fruits and sorbets that went into them and cold enough to induce the king of all brain freeze headaches. By substituting a few soda runs with a smoothie throughout the day I was able to reduce my soda consumption to a reasonable level (well reasonable for an addict, preposterous for a normal person). The Smoothie business was very cool, (yes that pun was intended). The demographics of my Smoothie customers and sandwich customers were very different. Most of my sub customers were college kids who wanted the most bang for their food dollar. They would come in to take advantage of my $4.00 foot longs after 4:00 p.m. promotion. Most of my lunch crowds were cubicle dwellers from the surrounding offices who wanted a quick meal for under $5.00. The smoothie crowd, however, was not as price sensitive as the sub crowd and anything more than a 20 ounce smoothie seemed foolish to them. They were more interested in the nutritional value of the smoothies and what nutritional supplements we offered to enhance their frozen concoction. The most bizarre and probably illegal smoothie we invented was called the "Drunken Eskimo." Some enterprising college students wandered in one evening from the bar next door. They asked if I had any alcoholic smoothies for their consumption. I told them that I didn't have a liquor license but would be happy to provide them a delicious smoothie that they could add their own enhancements to. They liked the idea and returned minutes later with their alcohol of choice. They would select their base smoothie, and while in the blender phase of production I would add their BYOB to create a unique "Drunken Eskimo" smoothie for their imbibement. For those of you that are offended by the term "Drunken Eskimo" and believe that this term is derogative and politically incorrect, I don't give a crap. Sorry for being so blunt and politically incorrect, but honestly, I don't give a crap. I don't know what any of this has to do with my soda addiction; I just thought it was an amusing sidelight to the main story.

We did however; try to integrate my affection for soda into the smoothie business. We tried various formulas to try and introduce the soda flavor to the smoothies. The closest we ever came was when we added the Coke syrup directly from the box, undiluted, to a smoothie. It wasn't bad but it wasn't a show stopper either.

I can't tell you just how much soda I consumed during those years but I am confident that it was way more than a human being should. I was often concerned about the potential impact this Coke addiction was having on my body. I rationalized that I knew it wasn't benefiting my health but I was confident that it wasn't damaging it. People would tell me "do you realize that that stuff is used to clean old coins? Think about what that is doing to your stomach." Well that is simply absurd. We are comparing apples to oranges here. It is a matter of bad versus badder (no, not bladder; badder; although either would work here). Sure, Coke can remove rust stains from porcelain or clean burnt pans or return your bathroom tile grout back to sparkling white, but can you imagine what stomach acid could do? We're not introducing Coke to some inanimate object here like a coin or bathroom sink that can't fight back. Once Coke enters our bodies, it's introduced into a cauldron of acid. I refuse to believe that Coke is a match for stomach acid. I can guarantee you that Coke doesn't have the debilitating effects on my throat and stomach that acid reflux does! Case closed, your argument stinks, pass me another Coke.

What soft drink has trademarked the slogan "Obey Your Thirst"?

Sprite is marketed with the slogan "Obey Your Thirst". The Coca-Cola Company first introduced sprite in 1961.

What soft drink was developed as an alternative to alcoholic beverages during prohibition?

IBC Root Beer was developed in 1919 by the Independent Breweries Company in St. Louis MO as an alternative to alcoholic beverages during prohibition.

The Coca-Cola bottle is modeled after the Cocoa Bean Pod, which has a similar bulging middle.

The site where Coca Cola was first bottled in Mississippi is now a fat camp for children. (No irony there!)

There are how many Coca-Cola themed museums in the United States?

It is believed there are at least 27 but we do not know for sure.

CHAPTER SEVEN

(OKAY, MAYBE I'VE HAD ENOUGH)

WHAT HAPPENED TO TAB?

I love TaB and I'm man enough to say it! I don't know what Coke does differently between Diet Coke and TaB, but given the choice between the two, I'm drinking TaB. I suspect that I'm not alone in that opinion, which raises the question, "what ever happened to TaB?" It just disappeared off the grocery store shelves. You see it pop up periodically in this retail esTaBlishment or another, but never with any consistency. Even the stores that carry TaB only dedicate a tiny portion of the display area for

TaB. I speculate that TaB's biggest obstacle to widespread acceptance was its association to women. In the same vein as pink shirts and jewelry, TaB had a feminine persona. I'm a 6'1", 220 lb., deep voiced hairy ape of a man oozing with testosterone who has no apprehension at all about sporting a can of TaB. I'm not intimidated by the threat of less secure men ribbing me or the occasional double take from a passerby. I love TaB and wish I had one of those gorgeous and delicious pink canned babies right now.

If I had to guess what ultimately turned the fate of TaB, I would have to focus on the Saccharin disaster. Chicken Little, we'll call him the U.S. Government, decided that saccharin was a carcinogen in laboratory mice and by extension was a threat to human beings as well. They didn't bother to tell us that the mice were consuming 500 times their body weight in this stuff on a daily basis. So it turns out that if I were to drink 3,552,000 cans of TaB a day over the course of my life time, I may get cancer. It all turned out to be hogwash but it appears that the damage was done. Of course this attack on TaB was two-pronged. Once they announced that Saccharin was a carcinogen, Coke introduced Aspartame as the sweetener in TaB. This obviously altered the taste characteristics of the drink, making it less attractive to its loyal fans. Do I have to remind anyone of the "New Coke" debacle? When you mess with a man's cola recipe, you better get it right and that is no easy feat. I'm not saying that it can't be done. Coke has been cranking out God's gift to mankind for over a century and one misfire with "New Coke" does not define a company's existence. I will tell you that Coke has recently pulled off just such a hat trick with the introduction of Coca Cola Zero. Oh yeah, this stuff is right on. Don't even get me started about Diet Cherry Coca Cola Zero. This is the stuff dreams are made of. Back to TaB.

TaB has evolved into a cult-like following. Diet Coke reigns supreme and TaB is but a distant memory. Back in the 1970's we always wondered just what TaB meant. None of us really knew for sure. The rumor was that it meant "Totally Artificial Beverage." Today's consensus is that it was just a computer exercise for the Coke marketing guru's trying to come up with a catchy four letter word. Coke had a state-of-the-art IBM 1401 computer (probably had less memory and processor speed than my wristwatch does today) and Coke's marketing department decided to put it to work. Why the name ultimately ended up three letters instead of four is anyone's guess, and why it's spelled TaB and not Tab or TAB may never be known definitively. Evidently back in the day at Coca Cola Enterprises, Coke was a sacrosanct word that was to be revered and protected. When someone recommended that the new diet cola be named "Diet Coke" they were accused of heresy and the idea was summarily dismissed without prejudice! My how things have changed! Here's a list off of the top of my Diet Coke filled head of Coke products of the past, present and future: New Coke, Coke II, Coke III, Diet Coke, Ultra Coke, Ultra Diet Coke, Coca-Cola Light, Coke Classic, Caffeine free Coca-Cola Classic, Caffeine free Diet Coke , Impulse Coke, Diet Coke Plus, Coca-Cola C2 , Coca-Cola C3PO, Shiso (I kid you not), Diet Coke Cherry, Coca-Cola with Lemon, Diet Coke with Lemon, Coca-Cola Vanilla, Diet Coca-Cola Vanilla, Coca-Cola with Lime , Diet Coke with Lime, Frosty Coke, Coca-Cola Raspberry, Diet Coke Raspberry, Boom Coke, Coca-Cola Black Cherry Vanilla, Diet Coke Cherry Vanilla, Coca-Cola

Blãk, OK Soda, Coca-Cola White, Jazz Coke and of course TaB, Lemon-Lime TaB, Black Cherry TaB, Ginger Ale TaB, Orange TaB, Strawberry TaB, Raspberry TaB, Rootbeer TaB, Lunar TaB, TaB with Calcium, TaB Energy, TaB Clear and Baobab.

Now the reality is that I conducted no research in the development of this book, hence, this could all be the senseless ranting of a Coke addict with no historical accuracy at all. I will readily admit that some of the names listed above are purely fictional. And one last thought, what was with that funky textured bottle TaB came in? What was up with that? TaB is so cool. I love that stuff. I'm starting to tear up just thinking about it. TaB, TAKE ME AWAY! P.S. Have you noticed the little play on the word TaB throughout the book? Absolute genius! Okay, maybe not genius but certainly reasonably bright! FINE, it was clever at best, losers!

Anna Eliza is the best-known wife of John Pemberton. However, John was married three times in his life. A confederate soldier killed his first wife during a raid of their homestead. He was married for a very short time after his return from the war but left his second wife for Eliza. (If you believe this drivel, I have an ill-gotten copy of Coke's secret formula to sell)

John sold approximately nine servings of the soft drink a day for a grand total of $50 the first year, which resulted in a net loss of $20 for the year.

The word "Supercalifragilisticexpialicocious" became so popular after the success of Disney's "Mary Poppins", Coca-Cola wanted desperately to use the term in their advertising. Unfortunately, Disney Theme Parks had signed an exclusive partnership with PepsiCo and the courts sent Coke packing.

Tapping the top of a shaken can of Coke will minimize the amount of spray when the can is opened by releasing carbon dioxide bubbles back into the liquid from the bottom and sides of the interior of the can.

CHAPTER EIGHT

THE APPLE DOESN'T FALL
FAR FROM THE TREE

There are things that every father wants to pass on to his children. There are tidbits of wisdom and lessons of life that can make his children's lives better. We've all had those heart to heart talks with our kids that were sometimes uncomforTaBle but always worth the effort. So what great lessons have I passed on to my boys? What timeless words of wisdom have they taken away from our relationship?

- BYOC, never leave it to chance that your host will have Coke on hand.

- Left over Coke from meetings or conferences is fair game. Gather it up and hoard it for yourself.

- Never eat at a restaurant that doesn't offer free refills

- Wave and honk at Coke delivery drivers on the outside chance you will distract them and cause an accident. Any product that leaves the truck and hits the ground is public property - aka fair game.

- Coke is a diuretic and should not be used to hydrate during extreme physical exertion. HOGWASH! Drink a ton of it, if you're going to go, that's the way to do it!

- When you meet a young lady, offer her a Coke on the first date. If she responds" No thanks, I don't drink the stuff", dump her. She can't possibly have other qualities that can offset her disregard for Coke.

- If a homeless person asks you for money, offer them a Coke instead. It will absolutely change their life.

- If your kid's little league team asks you to bring the juice boxes for the after-game party, bring Cokes instead. You'll be a hero, (don't listen to the other parents, they're idiots and just don't understand).

- If your IT department tells you not to drink your Coke around your PC because you may spill it and fry the system, remind them that according to your father's list of alternate uses for Coke, Coke can be used to repair solder joints on circuit boards.

- Always go for the largest available fountain drink offered, you will enjoy the additional soda and your price per ounce drops dramatically.

- Always choose the foam cup when given the choice. Fountain drinks hold up considerably better in foam cups than in paper or plastic.

- Wrapping a fountain drink cup with a napkin and inserting the wrapped cup into a second cup will eliminate the beads of sweat that drip off of the outside of your cup on a humid day.

My boys are eternally grateful for all of my wisdom I have imparted on them. Evidently there were some other topics that their friends' fathers had talked to their boys about that I had overlooked. Something about safe sex, say no to drugs, drinking and driving, sports, college, marriage and family. Boy I feel sorry for those other boys, getting short changed on the passing on of the old parental wisdom. I guess they will just have to figure it out as they go. Hopefully they will have a chance to read this book. Someone has to take responsibility for these kids' futures, I'll carry the burden.

As I alluded to earlier in the book, none of my children has inherited the Coke gene, for the most part. However, that doesn't mean they have not flirted with an addiction to this nectar of the Gods. We might as well start with my oldest and finish with the youngest. While living in Dayton Ohio, my mini-mart of choice was Speedway (in Wyoming - Flying J and Diamond Shamrock, California and Colorado- 7-Eleven, Missouri-7-Eleven and Casey's General Store, Florida - Suwannee Swifty, Ohio was Speedway, Texas - Stripes, Tetco and Speedy Stop, all bittersweet memories). With the advent of "pay at the pump", mini-marts struggled with how to balance convenience and driving sales on their high margin offerings inside the store. They understood that a discounted soda offering was the perfect loss leader to get customers to enter the store where they could entice them with a veriTaBle plethora of impulse items. Understanding the allure of a delicious, cold and cheap fountain drink, they built these beautiful, expansive fountain areas. These fountain machines sported as many as twenty separate heads dispensing twenty different offerings. Speedway introduced a rewards program where you could earn free product by accumulating points for all of your purchases. My brilliant idea was to give all of my children and my wife a rewards card so that every time any of us filled up our vehicles with gas or made a purchase inside, we would accumulate bonus points. I naively thought that I would be the sole beneficiary of the rewards that waited. I fantasized about the unlimited free soda rewards that would extend to infinity and beyond! I actually believed that I would never have to pay for another soda again. What I didn't anticipate was that my children would cash in the points for their own use, leaving me high and dry on the soda front. It turns out that Justin, son number one, had developed a morning ritual of a few hot off the roller rotisserie hotdogs and a 44 ounce Coke on his way to school. If you think I love my Diet Coke, that boy loved those rotisserie hotdogs! Between his morning stop, occasional slip out of school for lunch and his after school snack run, he was cleaning me out of bonus points. I was lucky to get one free soda a month! Knowing he was denying his father the ability to secure a free soda fix, he operated this as a clandestine operation. In my ignorant bliss I let the manager know how displeased I was with the inconsistency of the bonus point accounting system. I informed him that there were weeks when the balance would shift several hundred points out of my favor yet I had made no redemptions during that period. He promptly offered to make an inquiry to corporate and see if we couldn't get an itemized list of the activity on the card. When I received the itemized accounting of the cards activity, I immediately put two and two together and got one, son number one that is! The difficulty was that I had reached a dichotomy. I was mad as hell that the boy had circumvented my brilliant plan and at the same time felt as proud as a peacock. As I read down the list and saw the endless string of 44 ounce Cokes my eyes started to well up. The boy was a chip off the old block! I regained my composure and put on my authoritarian dad face and instructed Justin to knock it off. However, he was determined and put forth some compelling arguments in his defense. My defenses were breached and in a moment of weakness I compromised and told him an occasional foray into bonus point heaven was accepTaBle, after all he was contributing to the point total, but to deny his old man his free sodas was just wrong on multiple levels. I am happy to share with you that Justin grew up to be a healthy and happy young man who was able to escape the clutches of his early Coke addiction. He never endured the pain and humiliation of a soda poisoning or the embarrassment of thirty trips to the bathroom during a normal eight hour work day. Shoot, he's just as happy with a tall glass of tea as he is with a glass of Coke. As a matter of fact he drinks way more tea than he does Coke. It seems like every time I see him he has a tall glass of iced tea in his hand. When we go out to eat, iced tea again. Ball games, tea. Fishing, tea. Hot days, cold days, somewhere in-between days, tea again. OH CRAP! THE KIDS

NOT A COKE ADDICT, HE'S A TEA HEAD! A freakin tea head! I should have seen the signs; reduced concentration and coordination, euphoria, dry mouth, insatiable munchies. That's what happens when you are dealing with your own addiction. You are too consumed in getting your next fix than to notice your own child's addiction.

Casey, son number two, has devolved (well it is certainly not a plus) into a hard-core Diet Coke user. Casey is quite public about his addiction. He not only acknowledges his affinity for the bubbly brew, he wears it as a badge of honor. Casey esTaBlished his unique quality while attending Sinclair Community College. He would arrive for his 8:30 a.m. class with his 2-liter of Diet Coke in hand. Sensitive to the needs of the professor and the fellow students, he would skillfully twist the top of his 2-liter Diet Coke, to release the swoosh of carbonation prior to the outset of the class. Casey had previously made the tactical error of interrupting a professor with his ill-timed opening of a 2-liter of nectar and faced the harsh punishment of having his 2-liter confiscated and banned from all future sessions. After an entire semester without that tantalizing and invigorating concoction of goodness to kick start his brain, class was just a blurred assembly of random thoughts and memories which translated to incredibly poor application come test time. He needed the clarity and energy he derived from that morning jolt of 67.628046 U.S fluid ounces of Diet Coke. So he learned to adapt and overcome his professors' objection to this 2-liter of Diet Coke invading the sanctity of the schools haven of learning. Casey would arrive early and take a desk in the back row, preferably one of the corner seats. He would stealthily release the pent up carbonation by carefully positioning his giant banana hand over the cap, creating an acoustical barrier between the escaping gas and the eavesdropping audience. He would then slowly and skillfully release the gas in a controlled manner worthy of the most stringent scientific experiment. Unbeknownst to those around him, the carbonation was free and his morning fix of Diet Coke was poised and ready for consumption.

Now there is only so much one can do to minimize the impact of one drinking directly out of a 2-liter bottle in the middle of class. Casey would take an initial swig to clear his mind and gain his focus for the mental exercise which lay ahead. He would take short, tactical hits off of the bottle throughout the remainder of class as needed to maintain his focus until all that remained of the cornucopia of goodness was the empty , vacuous shell of a once vibrant and delicious 2-liter of Diet Coke. As impressive as this feat was, what really makes this exercise impressive was that the early class was only 50 minutes in duration. That's right folks; this hard core Coke addict would down his first 2-liter of the day, straight out of the bottle, in 50 minutes or less! This mountain of a man could hit a 2-liter bottle with the same tenacity and skill that normal men employ to tackle a mere 20 ouncer, much less a 16.9 ouncer.

On more than one occasion, Casey's Diet Coke addiction even put him at odds with the law. Dayton, Ohio is not well known for its inclement weather. You have never seen Dayton on the evening news in the aftermath of a category IV hurricane or recovering from a major earthquake. There has never been a mud slide or brush fire that threatened the city. The last major flood the city had was at the turn of the 20th century. However, an occasional winter storm can shut down the city. Casey and his college roommate were holed up in their rental house riding out a brutal winter storm. All of the roads were shut down and the police and sheriff's department had declared a state of emergency. What this meant was that the only vehicles allowed on the road were emergency vehicles and those who had a bona-fide reason to be out there. Replenishing your soda inventory to ride out the storm is not a bona-fide reason.

With snow so deep they couldn't even get the vehicle out of the driveway, they proceeded to dig their way out and prepare for the harrowing drive 2 miles down Smithville Road to Sammy's Food Mart. Sammy was hard core and they were confident he would be open. There was a lot at stake and both men were dedicated to seeing this mission through. So without regard for their safety and the law, they freed their Subaru all-wheel drive wagon from the clutches of the snow and headed off for Sammy's. To make a long story short, they didn't make it. The roads had not been plowed and the snow was too deep. They ended up abandoning their vehicle off the side of the street and hoofing it to Sammy's. It should be to no one's surprise that upon arrival at Sammy's, they found it closed. A four-mile round trip in the cruelest of weather for nothing. Now one would assume that this would be a lesson in common sense that these two Coke heads would remember and learn from, but think again! A few months later after the grip of winter had passed and the turbulent storms of late spring were emerging, the boys found themselves in a comparable quandary.

It was late May and a pounding thunderstorm was drowning the city. The storm drains were at capacity and the streets were beginning to flood. Cars were stalling right and left and being abandoned where they died. Intersections were especially cluttered with stalled cars lying around like discarded trash. There was no mandate by the police to stay home but any sane individual would understand the logic in it. An addict is anything but sane, logical, rational, or sensible. These boys needed some soda and they needed it now. Fortunately, Casey had recently replaced his 1990 Chevy Cavalier Station Wagon with a 4X4 Dodge Dakota, super cab, pick-up truck. With the high ground clearance and four wheel-drive, they were reasonably assured they would not face the same fate as the rainstorm had dealt others. They loaded into the Dakota and faced the raging thunderstorm around them. They proceeded through the flooded streets with the abandoned vehicles all about. They made a quick pit stop into Sammy's to secure a 44 ounce fountain before heading on towards the Kroger Supermarket to insure an adequate supply for the weekend. Despite the pounding rain and scorching lightning flashing all around them, the trip was a success. The boys felt a little guilty for not stopping and rendering assistance to some of the stranded motorists but they were on a much more important mission and couldn't be distracted by the misfortune of others. The 2- liters and 12 packs were secure and their weekend supply was in the house and chillin in the fridge; 2-liters in the kitchen fridge and cans in the mini-fridge strategically positioned on its perch atop the end **TaB**le, next to the couch. Now that was one fine display of interior decorating acumen!

We have all seen the commercials from fast food joints where the mom or dad whips through the drive-thru on their way home from work to grab some dinner for the family. The problem is that the well intentioned parent is enticed by the alluring aroma emitting from the acquired food and decides to try a small sample of the goods. They begin by nibbling on a few french fries and before they know it, the fries are gone and they are pulling into the driveway. They proceed into the house where they are greeted by a ravenous gaggle anxiously anticipating diving into those delicious fries. When the family discovers there are no fries, the bumbling parent makes up some lame excuse about the drive thru employee screwing up the order at which time they retreat from the kitchen and back into the car to make the return trip, secure the alleged missing fries and return home the hero. The problem is he/she must make the same trip back home with the scent of the hot fries waffling through their olfactory lobes and presto, the vicious cycle continues. Casey had to overcome a similar challenge while in my employ at the Blimpie Subs and Salad Restaurant near the University of Dayton. Casey's girlfriend, nickname LA, would occasionally request that at the end of Casey's shift he bring home a sub and a Coke for her. Casey was always happy to comply but was rarely successful in fulfilling her request. Casey was a Coke addict and the likelihood that he could transport that fabulous 32 ounce Coke without sampling the goods was unlikely. At first he would simply secure a 44 ouncer for himself and a 32 ouncer for LA. The expectation was that having a 44 ouncer for him would be sufficient to get him to LA's house without invading her 32 ouncer. How sad the delusions of a Coke addict can be. Casey would polish off his 44 ouncer in short order and find himself eyeing that remaining 32 ounce cache of carbonated indulgence. Casey would arrive at his destination in disgrace. His fondness for the bubbly ambrosia had once again won the day. Casey experimented with a myriad of tactics to overcome his inability to successfully transport his girlfriend's beverage to its ultimate destination. He tried 20 ounce bottles instead of fountain drinks. He tried omitting the straw in the hope that having to remove the lid and drink directly from the cup while driving would deter him long enough to reach his destination. He tried to convince LA to partake of one of the alternative selections like Sprite, Root Beer or Dr Pepper. It was a simple strategy, as Casey considered these alternatives repulsive and not fit for human consumption; he would find the inner strength to resist their temptation. It simply was not to be. I realize that the vast population of normal beverage connoisseurs cannot relate to this tale but I know it hits home with my fellow sodaholics.

Kyle is son number three. Kyle was the poor toddler who was introduced to the joy of a 32 ounce Big Gulp when he was still in diapers. The only way we could keep him quite during our trips between Colorado and Wyoming was by resting a 32 ounce Big Gulp next to his car seat and combining two straws to bridge the gap between that fabulous Diet Coke and his mouth. Now on the surface one might think his fate was sealed and he was destined to be a Diet Coke addict and I admit there were signs along the way to adulthood where this appeared to materialize. However, common sense and irrefuTaBle intestinal fortitude has emerged triumphant and Kyle has risen above the peer pressure and the influence of the "house of addicts" from whence he came.

Clearly the biggest challenge for Kyle revolved around his years at Blimpie but, unlike me and the fountain drinks, for Kyle it was the 20 ounce bottles. The only problem that I had with Kyle's propensity for 20 ouncers was the cost. My cost on a 32 ounce fountain drink was around .10 to .15 cents. My cost on a 20 ounce bottle was around .65 cents. Kyle grew tired of me riding him all day about how much his soda habit was costing me so he decided to take matters into his own hands. He noticed that he could purchase bottled Cokes cheaper retail at the grocery store than I was paying wholesale from Coke. Kyle proceeded to take the bull by the horns and took it upon himself to restock our cooler with the bargain bottles of Coke product. At first it seemed innocent enough so I stayed on the sidelines and let him do his thing. It wasn't until the customers started complaining that I was compelled to get involved. What Kyle had bought were 16.9 ounce bottles, not 20 ounce bottles.

It turns out that the beverage vendors use the different sizes to maintain better control of the market. In my case, Coke provided the cooler and fountain free of charge as long as I purchased my product from them. To verify that I had purchased the product from them, they only offered the 20 ounce bottles to their wholesale customers in the restaurant business and the 16.9 ounce bottles to the general public. When the delivery driver saw 16.9 ounce bottles in the cooler, Coke threatened to remove the cooler or convert the agreement to a monthly lease on the fountain and cooler. Customers were pissed because they were paying a $1.30 for 16.9 ounces and Coke was pissed because I was buying my product from Sam's Club and not Coke! What a freakin mess! I yanked all of the bottles out of the cooler and restocked it with 20 ounce bottles from the Coke driver. All of the 16.9 ounce bottles were stored in the back and used for catering orders and to feed Kyle's addiction. Moral of the story is that a Coke addiction can have negative consequences in ways you have never considered.

What country's currency depicts the King downing a bottle of Coca-Cola? (Hint: It is still in circulation today)

The Federated States of Microambrosia in the Pacific Rim.

The company that tried to sabotage the launch of TaB was the Doltish Beverage Company of Duncepac, Ohio. The company did not survive the scandal and closed its doors on December 5, 1964.

More soda is consumed annually in the United States than all other beverages combined! (Yes, that includes water!)

What was the original name of Dr. Pepper?

I don't know and I don't care, this is a book about Diet Coke.

Frank Robinson was John Pemberton's bookkeeper. Numbers weren't his only talent, he also had excellent penmanship and is the designer of the famous Coca-Cola logo still used today.

CHAPTER NINE

FROM JUNIOR EXEC.
TO PARK RANGER

As you may have noticed, I have not quite figured out what I want to be when I grow up. I sat down and listed every job that I've had since I was a little sprig of a pup (I have no idea what that saying is supposed to mean), shoveling snow in winter, mowing grass in the summer, and delivering newspapers year round. I have had 57 jobs in my 49 years on this earth and it is time to add number 58! I have one last story to share with you that may be a big surprise to Justin, son number 1, but I doubt it. If anyone can see through my facade as a man with his addiction under control, Justin can.

My last tale took shape approximately two, three, four (good God, I am such a slacker) years ago. After selling my restaurants in Dayton, Ohio my wife and I decided to move to the coastal community of Corpus Christi, Texas. The decision was the result of a tradeoff between my desire to relocate to Florida and my wife's desire to be closer to our Grandchildren. My wife asked me what was so compelling about Florida. I told her the weather and the Gulf of Mexico of course. She then asked if I could have both of those things and be closer to our Grandchildren, would I consider an alternative. Of course I agreed. She then scheduled a short vacation to Corpus Christi, Texas and as the saying goes, "the rest is history." Justin and Miranda are the proud parents of our grandbabies Katelin and Joseph. They reside approximately 3 hours drive from Corpus Christi. When we announced to the kids that we were moving to Corpus Christi, they agreed to follow suit. The wheels were put into motion for the big move to Corpus.

My intention with this glorious move to the sunny south was to settle back into a normal routine of nine to five and secure a job back in the world of cubicle dwellers and endless meetings. Once again my subsistence revolved around vending machines, 2-liters from home and never passing up the opportunity to snag a delicious and fresh fountain drink from an always available and convenient mini mart. Justin on the other hand wanted to break free from the routine of working nine to five and chose a path of entrepreneurship. He began to seek out potential business opportunities in Corpus. He came across a self-serve carwash that sparked his interest. The car- wash had gone through tough times and consequently fell into disrepair and vandalism. Justin was intrigued by the challenge of restoring all of the equipment and reopening the business. I had not yet come across suiTaBle employment and so it was not difficult to real me in. We acquired the carwash in anticipation of his relocation; unfortunately, two years later we are still working out the details to best make this move a reality. In the meantime, good ol' Dad is taking care of the daily tasks involved in operating the carwash. Long story short, we bought the car wash and in short order, had it fully functional and open for business. I naively believed that running this car wash would be enough to keep me occupied and out of trouble but it wasn't to be. I would tinker around in the morning hosing down wash bays, emptying the garbage and refilling the vending machines. I would collect up all of the quarters and refill the change machine. The whole affair would take less than an hour and the rest of the day was mine to screw off. I thought I was ready for a life of leisure but it was horrible. At first I would wander down to Corpus Christi Bay or head out to the national sea shore to do some birding but I couldn't do that every single day. I'm not a shopper so even Home Depot and Lowe's got boring after a while.

I decided to look into gainful employment again and came across a job as a buyer at an alumina refinery in neighboring Gregory, Texas. It was 9-5, Monday through Friday with no evenings or weekends and paid way more than it should, so I went for it. This is where the story unfolds. The carwash business makes its money twenty five cents at a time. At the end of every day when I empty the coin boxes, I collect 300, 400, 500 quarters at once. Yeah, that's right; a Coke addict has access to hundreds of quarters a day, ironically, the same denomination of coinage used in a soda vending machine. So let me clarify exactly what the situation is, the Coke addict is back in the cubicle world and he has an unlimited supply of quarters at his disposal to feed the office vending machine. Sure, the quarters do not technically all belong to me and are not mine to spend willy nilly as I see fit. Surely a son is willing to make this one little sacrifice to give comfort to his father's challenging environment of boredom followed by more boredom topped off with a third and fourth helping of boredom to finish off the day?

I'm not positive whether Justin actually knows this reality or not but I did let the cat out of the bag during one of our phone conversations. A customer had used a Mexican peso instead of a quarter in one of the vending machines at the car wash. The slug buster in the coin acceptor rejected the coin and captured it in the containment area of the acceptor. I retrieved the coin with the intent to save it as a novelty item. Unfortunately, I made the exact same mistake my customer had made and inadvertently attempted to use it in the soda machine at work. I thought this turn of events was humorous and shared the story with Justin. Justin's first response was "so you are spending quarters at work that you took from the carwash?" I began an aggressive tap dance where I explained that the only reason I had the peso on me was due to the novelty of the item. I explained that if it had been a quarter it would have been deposited into the bank with the rest of the money and would have never been in my possession in the first place. He responded, "Sure Dad, it looks like I've sent the wolf to guard the sheep." Well Justin, let us just say that your old man is one fat and happy wolf!

I have always been an over-achiever (that's my story and.....you know the saying) but I was determined just to go to work, keep a low profile and stay below the boss's radar. That lasted all of about 2 days and the old competitive juices flowed into hyper-drive and I was off and running. I proposed a Fitness Center for the plant, laid the ground work for a Purchasing Card (P-Card) system, introduced some metrics to measure our performance, implemented process improvements to streamline our operation and generate significant savings, and on and on. Needless to say, these efforts did not go unnoticed and within no time I was on the boss's radar. Long story short, after 18 months in the trenches, I leap-frogged multiple layers on the orgchart and was promoted to Business Unit Manager (BUM) of the Clarification Business Unit. There were five BUM's in the plant who served directly under the Production and Maintenance Directors, who served directly under the President of the company. You read that correctly, I went from lowly buyer to one promotion away from VP status in one giant leap! The job was high pressure and demanded a lot of my time. My first act as Clarification BUM was to order a mini fridge for the office. I was really into the new Coke Zero, so I filled that baby up to the brim with 16.9 ounce Zero's. It was sweet with one down side. The Coke Zero was a new thing and most folks had not yet tried one, which ineviTaBly led to their curiosity and inquiries. The discussion would usually progress as follows: "Is that new Coke any good?" I would reply "It is fantastic. I like it better than Diet Coke." We would continue the senseless banter until we would reach that awkward moment where it was clear that I either offer them one of my beloved Coke Zeros to satisfy their curiosity or look like a total ass and move on. I never had an issue with looking like an ass so all is well that ends well.

The BUM position paid six figures which made Mrs. Coke addict very happy. I, on the other hand, was not in it for the money. I felt like I had paid my dues in my working years and was committed to dedicating the last twenty years of my working life to something that I enjoyed doing and would have no regrets from once I finally retired. Working at the refinery was high paced, high stress and very dangerous. One Saturday morning, my lovely bride Jen and I were heading out to Wal-Mart to stock up on groceries. My Blackberry was going off every 30 seconds and I was getting noticeably irritated. Two minutes from the Wal-Mart, the Blackberry rings and it is my Operations Superintendent. He informs me that the filter floor is shut down and we are in jeopardy of cutting off the plant flow. The plant pushed through a million dollars of product per day. If my department is responsible for shutting down production, I'm costing the company a million dollars a day. NO PRESSURE THERE! I tell Jenny that our trip has to be postponed and I need to head back to work. It's not enough that I had already invested 80 hours in the joint that week, duty called.

That fateful phone call was my epiphany. I was in a place that I didn't want to be and working a job that I didn't want to do. After a week or two or three of soul searching, I gathered up enough courage to engage my spousal unit about my dilemma. I went to the fridge and extracted a 12-ounce can of backbone. I popped the top and swigged down 75% of that elixir of testicular fortitude. I sat down beside her on the couch and broke the news," Jen, I no longer want to work at the refinery. I am in the wrong job.... blah, blah, blah." She calmly responds, "so what is it that you want to replace your six figure salary with?" I proceed to take her all the way back to 1979. At the ripe old age of 18, just 6 weeks out of high school, we loaded up my 1962 Ford Fairlane with all of our earthly belongings, made a quick pit stop at the Justice of the Peace to swap nuptials, took a short detour to the corner pony keg for a case of Little Kings Crème Ale, and hit I-75 south to start our new lives in the Sunshine State. I reminisced about the years I spent working in the mail room for the Florida Department of Revenue and how I would head across the government complex every month to the Florida Fish and Game building to see if they had any job openings. Well, they never did, and eventually we packed up and moved back north. For several years I bounced around at various jobs trying to find my place in society. I worked at a printing factory cranking out the USA Today newspaper and various other sundry publications. I was a clerk at a King Kwik Convenience store working the graveyard shift where I spent the night running off drunks who acted like they were unaware alcohol sales ceased at 1:00 am EVERY FREAKIN' MORNING!

I eventually ended up selling housewares door to door like the old time Hoover Brush man. It was brutal. I would pitch at least 100 people a day in the hopes of selling to 20% of them. If I could bag just $5 per sale, I made a $100 a day. It was no easy chore wading through 80 negative responses, slamming doors and calls to the police to get to those 20 yeses. Eventually I had had enough and knew I couldn't keep up the grind any longer. Ultimately, I was able to escape this rut by when I raised my right hand, recited the oath to support and defend the constitution of the United States of America and started our wondrous travels as part of the USAF. By now I had mustered-up the courage to lay it all out there for Jen's consumption. I may not have found that dream job at Florida Fish and Game back in 1979 but I may have found it now. I announced, with certainty and resolve, that I wanted to apply for a Park Superintendent position with Texas Parks and Wildlife (TPWD). I had found the job on the TPWD website for Lake Texana State Park in Edna, Texas. Edna was approximately 150 miles north of Corpus Christi. What was Jen's first question? You guessed it, "How much does it pay?" Not a good place to start! My current salary was around $120,000 annually. A Park Superintendent with Texas Parks and Wildlife, $52,000 annually! Her initial reaction was, as you would expect. "Have you lost your freakin mind? What is this, your mid-life crisis? I worked my ass off for thirty years to get this house and I'm not moving to Green Acres just so you can get this out of your system." Well this drubbing continued for several days until she finally relented. My guess is that she assumed I wouldn't get the job anyway. How was I going to make the argument that my thirty years as a Security Policeman, Missile Launch Officer, Contracting Officer and business owner translated into the knowledge, skills and abilities listed for a Park Superintendent? I didn't really know how I would make the compelling argument so I started at the beginning. I copied the knowledge, skills and abilities listed on the job posting and began matching each requirement with something that I had accomplished in my past. My goal was to demonstrate that these skills were not unique to running a park but were skills any manager employs in the conduct of his duties, whatever those duties may be. When General Motors hired Ed

Whitacre, the CEO from AT&T, to save the company from bankruptcy, the first question the press asked him was "What do you know about making cars?" He replied "I don't know anything about making cars but I know a heck of a lot about running a business." Fourteen pages later, my Doctoral Dissertation on why I was qualified to be a Park Superintendent was complete. In a nutshell, to paraphrase the blunt but true words of Ed Whitacre, "I don't know anything about running a state park but I know a heck of a lot about managing organizations and people." I finished the application package and attached my dissertation and hoped for the best.

The best came to fruition and I was invited to the Region 3 headquarters in LaPorte, Texas. LaPorte was about 6 hours north of Corpus Christi. I headed up the night before the interview and checked into a La Quinta. I wanted to make sure that nothing derailed my transition from miserable to nirvana. I could just envision my driving around Houston aimlessly, an hour late for my interview and lost. I have come to terms with the fact that I am the worst navigator on the planet so I wasn't taking any chances. I woke up bright and early and made the trek across the street to Jim's "In and Out" Market to secure a 44-ounce fountain drink to get things rolling. Jim's fountain setup was primitive by modern standards and dispensed a rather unimpressive beverage. Despite its lack of effervescence and less than precise syrup to water to carbonation ratios, I immediately began to inhale that always long overdue, never can come early enough, better than sex, (sorry Jen but it is what it is) first of the morning beverage. By the time I got back to the room (a mere 6 minutes later) I had consumed the contents of my recently procured 44 but was far from satiated. Before getting showered and changed, I headed down to the vending machine to grab a 20 ouncer to refresh my drink. I transferred the contents of the ridiculously over-priced vending rip-off into the remaining ice of my 44-ounce foam cup and began my day. I headed for the Region Headquarters early to ward off any missteps, accidents, road closures, meteors, UFO's, or anything else that could potentially derail my goal. I arrived at the headquarters approximately an hour and 10 minutes early. I figured that I would make my way into the building around 15 minutes prior to my scheduled appointment, which left me almost an hour to kill. I remembered passing a 7-Eleven between the hotel and the headquarters, so I headed out to imbibe on one more refreshing beverage before facing the life changing opportunity that lay before me. Just as a side note, 7-Eleven is a beacon of soda Mecca's among the masses of convenience store choices. I admit that you can occasionally come across some inferior locations but 7-Eleven consistently exceeds my expectations for cleanliness, selection and value. (How was that Mr. Depinto? Good enough to fulfill our covert, unethical, biased, and immoral agreement to shamelessly promote your stores in exchange for a life time supply of free fountain drinks? CRAP, did I think that out loud? I assure you that everything I have written here is from the heart with no outside influences or kickbacks from 7-Eleven lobbyists.) I digress which should not surprise you at this juncture. I returned back to the region headquarters with my always delicious and fresh 7-Eleven fountain drink in hand and reviewed my notes and other research material in preparation for the interview. I was about 10 minutes out before I was prepared to head into the building and begin to wow them with my brilliance, when my kidneys began sending the processed soda to my bladder for evacuation.

The last thing I wanted to do was dance through an interview preoccupied with whether or not I would have an incontinent moment! I decided to head in early to vacate my bladder so that I would not be distracted during the interview. I was gathering up my notes and suit coat when there was a tap on my car window. Darn near vacated my bladder right there! I looked up to see a baby faced young man, tall and fit, standing at the car window looking like someone who had something to say. As I opened the car door, I heard him ask "Are you Jeff?" I cheerfully replied, "That depends on who's asking............. IRS, ConsTaBle delivering a subpoena, friend, or foe." The youngster extended his right hand and eagerly introduced himself as Justin Rhodes, the Region 4 Director and my host for the next few hours. We exchanged pleasantries and Justin then invited me in to get things started. At this point I was not comforTaBle taking a detour to the restroom so I made the piss poor (pun intended) decision to commence the interrogation with a full bladder. I figured I had done it hundreds of times on long trips, this would be no different.

I gathered up my things and headed into the building following behind Justin like a little puppy. We navigated our way through the maze of cubicles, stopping at every stinking one to exchange introductions and engage in senseless banter as if we were long lost friends catching up on all of the events which had transpired in the intervening time. I played the game like a seasoned pro and executed every exchange as if my future depended on it. We finally made it to the interview room where I met the other four panel members. To make a long story short (it is always a moot point by the time I say that isn't it?), I never made it the distance and interrupted the interview an hour into it to make a beeline for the can. I made a joke of it referencing my advanced age of 48 and my enlarging prostate as the likely cause. Luckily all of the panel members were men and found a sliver of humor in it. Despite my inability to control my soda addiction for just one stinking morning so that I could focus on the task ahead and land my dream job, despite the embarrassment, despite my preoccupation with pissing my pants instead of nailing the questions they were throwing at me, I WAS HIRED!

My first task as the newest Park Superintendent for Texas Parks and Wildlife was to attend the Managing Park Operations School held at one of the TPWD parks, the Parrie Haynes Ranch. Parrie Haynes was a remote park nestled deep in the foothills about 40 miles west of Austin, Texas and about 30 miles south of Killeen, Texas. The physical distance from civilization is not what made the ranch so remote. It was the narrow, dirt roads that wound through the foothills up to Parrie Haynes that made it so remote. I would be staying in a cabin with no refrigerator and no opportunity to stockpile an adequate soda supply for my 3-week stay. I knew there would be a few days of mind splitting headaches as I detoxed from my soda addiction, but I figured it was a great opportunity to kick the habit once and for all. Before committing to the three-week excursion, I passed the turnoff to Parrie Haynes and headed into Killeen to ingest as many Diet Cokes as I could without facing the dreaded and always near fatal soda poisoning. I sucked down two 32 ouncers at McDonalds and then stopped into 7-Eleven on my way out of Killeen. I snagged a 64-ounce fountain and two 20-ounce bottles for good measure.

I turned off the main highway and began my ascent to Parrie Haynes Ranch. As I approached the entrance to the park I thought I saw a small sign that said "Welcome to Camp Coca Cola." I spun my head around for a better look but I had already passed the sign. It was starting to get dark so I assumed I had misread the sign. I was worried that just the anticipation of the ineviTaBle detox that awaited me was causing premature hallucinations. I was concerned how this might affect my ability to successfully complete the school. It had taken me 30 years and a lot of wrong turns to get here and I didn't want to blow it! Luckily I hadn't consumed either of the two twenty ounce bottles of Diet Coke I had secured on my way out of Killeen. I strategized how I could utilize this surreptitious soda to its utmost potential in staving off the effects of my impending detox. I contemplated how much soda a day I would have to consume to fool my body into believing that soda deprivation was not at hand. Maybe a few gulps in the morning and one more in the late afternoon would be just enough to keep me on the edge of withdrawals. The pop will be warm, which is disgusting, but even warm soda is better than no soda. Heck, it's worth a shot!

I arrived at the lodge where we were scheduled to check in for our cabin assignments and further instructions. I tore up the entrance steps two at a time, as I was overwhelmed with anticipation for what lie ahead. Now understand that I was not as young as I once was. I stood at the top of the stairs for a minute or two, bent over and sucking wind and gasping for any molecule of oxygen I could muster. Recovered enough to proceed, I entered the lodge. The breathtaking beauty of its interior immediately took me in. I was admiring all of the beautiful wood, the exposed beam ceiling, rustic furniture and pine log walls when my attention was abruptly redirected to the wall immediately above the kitchen double doors. Hanging above the doors was a sign that read "Camp Coca Cola." I KNEW IT! I KNEW I HAD SEEN THAT SIGN EARLIER. I KNEW I WASN'T HALLUCINATING! So now I knew I wasn't going nuts but the question still lingered, why was this place called Camp Coca Cola? Had I arrived in heaven? Was the culmination of my life dream really just karma uniting me with my one true love on this earth, Diet Coke? Was all of the soul searching, sleepless nights, manipulation of my poor spouse, just fate's way of bringing me home? Probably not, but it is a pretty cool coincidence! I decided that the mystery of Camp Coca Cola would have to be solved at a later time so I ventured out to find the TaBle to check in, when out of the corner of my eye, I spotted that radiant luminescence of scarlet and white. That always familiar and comforting swoosh, as white as the driven snow, against the fire engine red backdrop, a Coca-Cola fountain machine! I turned to see and BAMM! Two freaking soda fountains! One fountain each standing like bookends on each side of the entrance. How in the hell did I miss that? Why weren't my Coke senses tingling out of control as I entered this Shangri-La? I was about to find out and it wasn't going to be pretty.

Yes I was excited. Yes it was of orgasmic proportions but something just wasn't right. I took a deep breath and gathered myself. As I approached the soda fountains I sensed a major calamity of biblical proportions looming. I stopped about twelve feet from the fountain immediately to the right of the entry and stared. I was looking for anything out of place, anything that might tell me the current status of the equipment. Were there signs of life? Was there evidence that they were indeed fully operational or just relics from some former life? Everything seemed to be in order so I stepped a few feet closer when I noticed the first fountain head was labeled "Hi-C Orange Drink." The second head, "Hi-C Orange Drink." The third head, fourth head, fifth head... ... ...AAAAUUUUGGGGHHHH!! I immediately looked to the left at the other fountain station, more desperate for a favorable outcome than at any other moment in my life, but it was not to be. Camp Coca-Cola had two soda fountain stations each with six marvelous dispensing heads and ALL DISPENSING Hi-C ORANGE DRINK! Really? I mean freakin' really!!! You know a lesser man would not have survived such a crushing defeat but for a hard core addict, this was just another bump in the road. Over the past 30 years I have been to the highest mountain top and lower than a bullfrog's naval. Chalk this up to just one more ride on the addiction roller coaster. I later found out that Coca-Cola maintains a corporate office in Austin. This office donated the funds to construct all of the cabins and the dining facility at Parrie Haynes Ranch. In exchange, TPWD granted Coca Cola one-week every year to hold their corporate retreat at, you guessed it, Camp Coca-Cola where there's no damn Coke the rest of the year!

Well folks, I think I've ridden this gravy train as far as she'll go, so I'll wrap this up. I believe my relationship with Texas Parks and Wildlife is the last occupation I will have. I spend every day at work, where everyone else comes to on the weekends and holidays to get away from work. That's a pretty good gig. Sure, the pay stinks and my poor wife gave up her beautiful home in Corpus Christi for government housing in the middle of Green Acres but it beats the heck out of a cubicle or even a corner office. This book has been a true labor of love to write. I hope you enjoyed it and saw plenty of your own life sprinkled in here and there. Call, email, meet for lunch, or invite over everyone you know and turn them on to this incredible story. You are absolutely forbidden from lending them your copy of the book. Give them a few hits for free. Read them a few passages just to whet their appetite. When they come back for more, kindly direct them to the nearest bookseller or Amazon.com and BAMM I am in the money! After all, it is all about me.

Coca-Cola was originally marketed for its medicinal qualities.

Coca-Cola holds over 162,471 beverage patents in 64 countries around the world

Most everyone is familiar with the major anniversary themes: 25th is silver, 50th is gold, 75th is diamond and 100th is platinum. What most people don't know is the first 10 years are all Coca-Cola and years 51 - 74 and 76 - 99 are all Diet Coke.

As of 2010, at least 159 direct descendants of John Pemberton were employed at rival soft drink manufacturers.

The TV movie, "The Bengal and the Cincinnati Kid" was inspired by what soda?

Do I really need to tell you at this point in the book? Fine, it was Diet Coke, duh.

CHAPTER TEN

(ALTERNATE USE #1)

ALTERNATE USES FOR COKE

- Clean a toilet

- Dissolve a styrofoam cup in 7 hours

- Removes labels and glue residue better than Goo Gone

- Remove rust from chrome and other sundry metals

- Whiten teeth

- Clean corrosion from car battery terminals:

- Loosen a rusty bolt

- Bake a moist ham

- Bake a dry ham

- Dissolve a human tooth in 24 hours

- Coca-Cola (Original Coke exclusively) will help loosen grease stains from any material/surface

- Clean road haze from your windshield

- Dissolve a nail in about 4 days

- Clean truck engines

- Clean car engines

- Clean any kind of engine

- In many states (in the USA) the highway patrol carries two gallons of Coca-Cola in the truck to remove blood from the highway after a car accident.

- Used in the IT world to repair solder joints on circuit boards

- Dissolve a T-bone steak in about 2 days

- Relieving jelly fish stings

- Treat wasps stings

- Curling hair

- Cleaning pots

- Treats acne

- Cleaning oil spills off the garage floor

- Minimizes "crows feet" and other fine lines

- If you leave Coke exposed to the air for 8-12 years (depending on climate factors) it will eventually turn into a substance harder than a diamond

- Create fake antique photos

- Dissolves cellulite

- A sealed can of Coke sinks in water but Diet Coke floats

- Relieving constipation

- Strips dye from hair

- Kills dandelions

- Repels mosquitoes

- Etches concrete

- Removes scuff marks from floors

- Skin softener

- Tanning Lotion

- Scott Adams "Dilbert's" beverage of choice

- Add to washer to remove odors

- Secret ingredient of Gorilla Glue

- Considered an enhancement drug in the Olympics

- Nail polish remover

- When flat (no carbonation) prescribed by doctor's as a colon cleanser prior to a Colonoscopy

- Used as a herbicide to kill invasive plant species in lakes, ponds and rivers (not effective on land)

- Rodent exterminator (they are attracted to the sweet nectar but cannot expel gas so they explode!)

- When freeze dried makes an nutritious chicken feed

- Better than lacquer thinner when mixed with Fresca

- When combined 2:1 with gluten and heated to 87 degrees Fahrenheit, creates an exceptional depilatory

- Removes dark rings under eyes

- In mist form, provides outstanding stain resistance to carpets and fabrics

- Treats sunburn

- Treats poison ivy and poison oak

- Will **_not_** dissolve an aspirin (aspirin are impervious to Coke for which scientist have no explanations)

- Can be used to supplement ink in laser printers

- Clean dry erase boards

- Secret ingredient in Rogaine (responsible for the thick, luxurious characteristics of the newly grown hair)

- Superior glass cleaner when diluted with green Kool-Aid

- Main ingredient in the soap used to wash UPS trucks

- Used in the first generation satellites as a coolant/antifreeze

- Did I mention it was Dilbert's beverage of choice?

- Effective wood preservative in elevations above 6000 feet

- Exceptional pottery glaze (especially brilliant when kiln fired above 2840 degrees)

- Conan O'Brien's hair gel (Original Coke exclusively and is only effective on red, strawberry and platinum blonde hair. Original Coke is moderately effective on towheaded, sandy, and golden blondes Definitely not effective on venetian, honey, dirty, or dishwater blondes. Ash-blondes are hit or miss, bottle blondes...FORGET ABOUT IT!)

- Boosts rattlesnake anti-venom's effectiveness

- Freeze dried Diet Coke is used in baseball rosin bags

- Fish attractant (marinate bait overnight in Regular or Diet Coke)

- Only known product that cleans fiber optics without damaging it

- Used in the former Yugoslavian province of Slobavanskuptula to stain and preserve soft woods like pine and several varieties of firs

- I love Dilbert and he loves Diet Coke (I'm just saying)

- Tans leather

- Great spray starch (dark clothing only)

- Kills mold and mildew

- Absorbs odors

- Effective lubricant and spermicide

- Watercolor paint that will never fade or run

- Embalming fluid (but not cost effective)

- Furniture polish and scratch remover

- Used in swimming pools to boost chlorine's effectiveness

- And probably the least known use for Coke is that it is used in manufacturing as part of the "Bayer Process" to extract alumina from bauxite.

As you may have already determined, this list is as fictitious as my whole premise of being a Coke addict. Thank you for buying this book, the proceeds will help put my fictitious three sons through college and supplement my fictitious Air Force pension. Drink on!

Who holds the world record for the most ounces of Coca-Cola consumed in 2 minutes as listed in the Guinness Book of World Records?

I do not know if there is such a record but there should be and whoever sets the record should be a national hero!

How many ounces of Coke are sold every day around the world?

How the heck would I know as long as I have mine! You are on your own to research this useless tidbit of crappola.

Coca-Cola made its debut in cans in what year?

1955

What beverage was Coca-Cola's biggest failure? (Hint: not the "New Coke" debacle of the 1980's)

Apesta rolled out on March 1, 1927 to tremendous fanfare and anticipation until it was discovered that "Apesto" translates to "Stinks" in Spanish. Coke tried to launch a damage control campaign but it was too late. They became the laughing stock of the world in 1927.

"Mr. Dilbert you are suffering from a severe case of soda poisoning. We are going to   attempt a **Soda Dialysis**. Nurse, we are going to need a ice machine, and a 64 ounce cup **STAT!!!**"

Justin Dilbert

CONCLUSION

Writing "My Life as a Coke Addict" has been a true labor of love (advance sales have been very promising). I have consumed massive quantities of Diet Coke in the process, strengthening Coke's market share and shoring up its stock value. I spread the wealth among 2-Liters, 20 ounce bottles, 16.9 ounce bottles, and 12 ounce cans as well as many, many 32 and 44 ounce fountains. For all of you that see a little bit of yourself in some of these stories, I hope I have provided you some comfort in knowing that you are not alone in your addiction. There are certainly worse vices we could be burdened with than a soda addiction (that's my story and I'm sticking to it).

I have run out of stories and have humiliated my family and myself enough so I will bid you all a heartfelt, albeit disingenuous, farewell.

STOP THE FREAKIN' PRESSES! STOP THE FREAKIN' PRESSES! STOP THE FREAKIN' PRESSES! STOP THE FREAKIN' PRESSES!

What an unbelievable turn of events (as if any of this drivel has been believable). Recently I have found myself struggling with the simplest mental functions. I no longer remember peoples' names and often struggle to find that right word in a normal conversation. I am only 49 years old so Alzheimer disease and dementia are unlikely culprits. Over the past six months, I have broken four fingers, my wrist, and most recently fractured my foot. The doctor was ……..(oh what am I trying to say here?) (See, I told you) justifiably concerned and decided to run a few tests. He began with a bone density test and determined that my flesh, muscles, and organs are now supported by balsa wood. My bones have the density of a bird. As for my diminishing mental functions. What? Oh right, my diminishing mental functions, my doctor referred me to a specialist who launched a massive series of apparently non-reimbursable tests for someone of my age group, at least according to my insurance company. The specialist concluded that my symptoms did not fit any of the typical earmarks for Alzheimer's or dementia and is likely being caused by some external, environmental factor. I am now bankrupt, mentally in a fog, and precariously unsTaBle on my brittle frame as I return to my primary physician for some guidance and advice. The doctor is baffled and decides to proceed with a regimen of regularly scheduled lab tests and follow-up visits in an attempt to pinpoint the cause of my decline. I returned a few weeks later to have my blood drawn and to deposit a urine sample. After a short face to face with the doc, I head back to work. Later that afternoon I get a call from the lab. An overtly agitated lab technician informs me that my practical joke was not appreciated and that I will need to provide a valid urine sample. Being in a fog the overwhelming majority of the time these days, I'm not processing what the technician is telling me. I respond "huh"? She continues, "Ha-ha, real funny, I have nothing better to do than to process a sample a Diet Coke." I respond "huh"? She continues, "The urine sample you submitted is just Diet Coke and you are still liable for the charges associated with processing it and we still need a legitimate urine sample". I assure her that I have no knowledge of this and it certainly is not a prank. I have no explanation as to why the sample did not contain any urine but I would be happy to provide another sample. You guessed it; this went on for two more iterations before Dr. Nyugen got involved. I sat in Dr. Nyugen's office and assured him that I was not up to any shenanigans. I suggested he observe me dispensing the next urine sample to validate that it came from my own stinking bladder. As I filled the specimen jar, for the first time ever, I noticed the dark, rich, caramel color of my urine stream. And, for the first time ever, I noticed the effervescence bubbling up in the jar. Dr. Nyugen looked in amazement and told me that this was very concerning and likely is the key to all of my maladies. Let me wrap this up for you - after my life-long addiction to Diet Coke and my unprecedented volume of consumption, it appears it has had a profound effect on my body. The Diet Coke that I consume simply bypasses all normal digestive functions and passes directly through to my bladder where it not so patiently awaits repulsion, I mean conviction……………….or maybe discharge. No that sounds too much like an STD. Focus, focus, expulsion! Yes, expulsion makes sense. God this is torture! It also appears that on its way through my body, it absorbs all the vitamins, minerals, nutrients, and calcium that it encounters. The good news is that the discharged Diet Coke is an incredibly potent and vitamin enriched version of Diet Coke. What it tastes like is yet undetermined (for obvious reasons!). The bad news is that it leaves a vitamin and mineral deprived blood stream to service my organs, specifically, my brain. Oxygen is displaced by carbonation rendering my brain, rendering my brain, rendering my brain, rendering my brain, less than optimal. It would be like putting 87-octane fuel in a jet engine.

My only motivation for writing this book was to make a little scratch. As it turns out, I am a hot commodity for the science world. I have turned over my body to science and the Coca-Cola Company, to dig, probe, cut, radiate, poke, prod, and violate, all for an insanely outrageous amount of money. The way I see it, I'm more stupiderest, more dumberer, more dim, thick, dense, slow, and dim-witted by the day. My balsa bones are snapping like twigs, with no way to reverse the damage. I don't know how much time I have left, but while I'm here, I literally have Diet Coke running through my veins. What more could a coke addict ask for? I will make this commitment to you, if the doctors and scientist complete their case study prior to publication of this book............................ lost my train of thought, give me a second. If they complete the study before this book is published, I will include the results in the book. I no longer need the money, but the stupid book is finished now, it seems ridiculous not to publish it. Ahhhh, Diet Coke IV's are heaven on earth.

Drink on! I'm sure you are in no danger of facing the same fate as me. Even if you do, by then science will have a solution, allowing you to drink to your heart's content. Simply pop a pill and viola, good as new. It should be out right after the fat pill and the cure for the common cold. Trust me. I'm an addict. I always tell the truth.

THE END

In what country was the Coca-Cola polar bear first used in an advertisement?

Who would have guessed France? I did not realize France was first at anything, ever, well unless you are talking surrender. (Well there goes any hope of selling this book to the French)

What do Dr. John Pemberton (founder of Coca-Cola) and James E. Casey (founder of United Parcel Service - UPS) has in common?

They were high school buddies that started the Solvent Cream Application for Trucks Company or "S C A T" in 1882. They invented a superior soap and polish using John Pembertons original Coca-Cola syrup recipe. John and James parted ways, as there was no real application for their product in 1882. James was smart enough to patent the soap. UPS still uses SCAT today, which is why their trucks are brown and always impeccably clean!

What was the first soft drink consumed in outer space?

In July of 1985, Coca-Cola became the first soft drink consumed in outer space. It was enjoyed by astronauts aboard the Space Shuttle who sipped the soda from a specially designed "space can".

In Japan, there is a market for cola-flavored cigarettes called "Little Bobdog Coca-Cola Cigarettes" complete with Disney-style characters on the boxes.

What was Coca-Cola originally called?

More eerie than a Nostradamus prophecy, it was called "Jeff's Drink" named after the founders eldest son, Jefferson P. Davis Cumquat Junior Pemberton III.

Some memorable and not so memorable TaB advertising tag lines: "Body by TaB", "Fuel to be Fabulous", "Pink Power", "For Chicks and Dudes Alike", "TaB - For Beautiful People", "Pinkalicious", "Generation TaB", "Totally Amazing Beverage",

TaB made its public debut on April fool's day 1963

There are three places in the United States that still have laws on the books prohibiting the sale of Coca-Cola. The laws were enacted in the 1800's when Coca-Cola contained cocaine. What are they?

Waspich County, LA., Puritanical, RI., and Hackneyed, GA.

The Coca-Cola logo is the most recognized corporate logo in the worls and is universally recognized in every corner of the planet.

The "New Coke" recipe from the 1980's was not a disaster everywhere. Where was the "New Coke" a huge hit?

In an alternate universe maybe! Sure as heck nowhere in this world!

Coca-Cola product placements have been discovered in over 143,000 children's cartoons.

Coca-Cola products are served in over 85% of US high schools and 65% of US middle schools.

I really enjoyed totally fabricating all of the trivia you have read throughout this book. Please erase all of it from you gray matter or your next performance during a trivia based game could go horribly wrong.

John Pemberton created the original cola formula at his drugstore in Columbus, Georgia. The original concoction was a coca wine called Pemberton's French Wine Coca. It is speculated that Dr. Pemberton was inspired by the European coca wine, Vin Mariani.

What soda was invented at "The Old Corner Drug Store' in Waco, Texas?

I'm a Pepper, You're a Pepper, Be a Pepper, Drink Dr Pepper

6298502R00062

Made in the USA
San Bernardino, CA
05 December 2013